A Gathering of Shadows

A Gathering of Shadows

a novel by
Bob MacKenzie

Dark Matter Press
Kingston, Canada

Library and Archives Canada Cataloguing in Publication

MacKenzie, Bob, 1947-

A gathering of shadows / Bob MacKenzie.

Issued also in electronic format.

ISBN 978-0-9916858-0-6

I. Title.

PS8575.K424G38 2012   C813'.54   C2012-903580-7

for a long distant son
lost but not forgotten:
may he someday return
to those who love him

Special thanks to **Annie MacKenzie**
who took the author photograph
which appears with the biography
and to **Dorothyanne Brown**
who wrote the author biography

Any startling piece of work has a subversive element in it, a delicious element often.

— Leonard Cohen

My goal has been to approach the thriller or the horror field as a wide-open type of fiction that most writers have not treated seriously. It is a total joy for me to explore these genres and take them in directions they hopefully haven't been taken before and treat them with a seriousness that I believe they deserve.

— David Morrell

Now, in the silent half-light before dawn
she sits quietly waiting for something,
unaware of what she expects to come
as dawn's mist obscures the beasts in the dark.

The soft turquoise of her nightie wraps her
but doesn't stop the chill mists of the night,
cold fingers of the dead touching her skin
with soft caresses calling her to come.

Still, in the silent half-light before dawn
she sits and feels a shiver take her over
and she can't tell if it's from chill or fear:
around her, she senses the night dying.

Chapter One

Janice wonders how she got here. She stands at the rail. She looks out in every direction. Nothing. Only this part of a bridge. Or so it seems. The mist is very heavy for spring in Windsor. What time of day is it? Janice thinks early morning. Something to do with the light. And the shadows stretching across the mist swirled roadway. She is not sure.

She turns from the railing. At the edge of the mist she sees a man. He has something: a box or chest of some sort. As the mist clears for a second, then swirls back, she sees it is Rick. She starts toward him. She tries to call his name. She cannot speak. As she nears him, he opens what she now sees is a casket. From the opening, a rainbow. Around Rick, the rainbow. Rick is the rainbow. Bright. Colourful. Fading. Gone.

Only the bridge.

Janice hears something. An animal perhaps, in the mist. Moving toward her. She should be afraid. She is not. It is quiet. Like the purring of a gigantic cat. It is in the mist at what she assumes must be the Windsor end of the bridge. If the end of the bridge is even there. It grows louder, closer. Janice watches. Something is appearing from the haze. Not a cat. A car. How strange, Janice thinks, a car on a bridge with no beginning and no end.

It is a different car, very sleek and low, with a lot of chrome. The bottom of the body is red but the top is white. The chrome that separates the two colours is shaped like a lightning bolt, and it seems to glow with a blue fire. The roof is red. Across the roof, from side to side, circling roof and windows like a wedding band, is a wide,

1

sparkling chrome strip. The car purrs up to her and stops. There is no driver.

As though she had blinked her eyes in bright sunlight, there is a dancing rainbow of coloured light where the driver should be. She reaches to touch it. She is in the car. The rainbow becomes a driver, a good looking blond man she has never seen before. The car is chasing something, no! Somebody! It is the rainbow. It is Rick! Running, dodging. The car as agile as an ocelot she had seen in some film. She remembers the ocelot wins the chase: looks backward, not bearing to watch.

Behind, a man is chasing the car. Running! He looks like he is running: no sound. He looks like the driver. Something is wrong. She must get out. Open the door: find the handle, pull, push, fall.

Through the mist. Above, the bridge, and the man chasing the car chasing the man, all growing further and further. Falling with her, beside her, the box that holds the rainbow. Open the lid. Colour flow in lively profusion from the casket. There is the rainbow.

There is no rainbow. All colour is gone. All memory is gone. There is only grey, misty grey. And: there is the bridge. The bridge only. And only part of the bridge....

It all begins and ends again, and always the Janice on the bridge remembers none of it. But the other Janice, the one who watches, sits, her hands slimy with popcorn, through who knows how many showings, and remembers as well as a Rocky Horror freak. Finally, the house lights up; she wakes with a start: the sun rising. Her hands are slimy with sweat and her first look at morning sun has left a display of blue dots dancing before her eyes where her husband should be. She is alone.

Chapter Two

In that breathless pause between dark and dawn when the world seems void and lifeless and the city only threatens to exist, two men, strangers to each other, have become bound by the shadows of the night. Steve Lansing sits, unable to sleep, in the bay window of his inexpensive Riverside Drive apartment watching the murk of the Detroit River grow red with morning. Further west, Rick Bergeron is driving his cab back to the company garage on University Avenue. In each mind the questions have begun to grow.

Chapter Three

On the fifth floor of the almost deserted municipal parking garage the car sat in sleek contrast to the concrete surrounding it, the blue light from the street below glimmering in muted glows from the nickel silver lightning flashes separating the body into red and white, the chrome crown drawing a tiara of stardust across the red roof. Even after thirty years this Victoria looked nearly new. The motor purred contentedly to her sister, the night; the car was empty. So it sat for nearly a half hour.

The whisper of tires on gridded concrete and the low rumble of a winter worn muffler heralded the arrival of a second car. A blue and yellow taxi entered level five and, after a negligible pause, snuggled close to the ancient Ford. A minute passed, then two. Rick turned off the motor and stepped out. He was uncertain what to do next.

This was the fifth or sixth time Rick had taken one of these so called "specials": courier trips arranged by Lucio Atracura, the owner of six cabs operating under contract to Windsor Taxi, including the car Rick was now standing beside. This was the only time he had found only an empty car, the motor still running, at his destination. Usually these special trips had been quite easy and very lucrative. Usually it had been some booze or maybe some pot or hash: simple, move the goods from one place to the other and pick up a sizeable tip! It would go like clockwork. Bud, which was the Canadian name Lucio preferred, would catch a driver as he let off a fare, pass him two addresses and, if necessary, some money, and

4

leave. Bud owned the cabs; who could be suspicious if he checked up on his drivers once in a while? Even the company did not suspect.

This time was different. Bud had been very careful to describe the old car with the Michigan plates. He had been very careful to tell Rick to take care. This time there was nothing written; this time the money came in a sealed envelope, a big sealed envelope. Rick had been tempted, but he had not tried to open the envelope. Still, this time was different. Rick shivered. It was more than the chill spring breeze crossing the river from Detroit. There was something else.

Three rows deeper in the shadows of the parking garage one of the shadows, catlike, disengaged from the rest, moving silently toward Rick. The dusky wraith gradually resolved itself into the form of a man in bluejeans and a light leather jacket, his blond hair close cropped. One hand hung by his side but the other was raised to the level of his waist. The taxi driver, who had been lost in thought, gazing across the tops of stores and hotels, across the dark river toward the glitter of the Renaissance Center, turned.

The blond man's waist level hand swivelled toward Rick and Rick noticed what it held. He raised his hands. The blond man checked for weapons and, finding none, opened the trunk of his Ford.

The taxi driver handed over the envelope and received a cardboard carton about two feet square and wrapped in brown paper. The blond man pointed to the darkness he had walked from and the driver nodded understanding. The red and white Victoria slipped down the ramps and into the darkness of the streets below; the taxi driver got into his car but did not leave for nearly an hour. Then he left the parking garage to the blue light and the shadows, feeling still that, somehow, this trip was different. A lot different.

***

At the Pitt Hotel closing time was slow coming. Last call had come and gone and still the bulk of the denizens—the homosexuals and the lesbians, art and drama students from the university soaking up subculture, undercover cops and the lone reporter—held on to the party atmosphere engendered by the combination of spring and beer. A man stepped from the side door, recognized the pressure of too many beers drunk too soon after one another, and turned to regain the Pitt's washrooms. Too late! The door was locked. He glanced at the street. It was too open, too visible. He looked some more. There, kittycorner to the Pitt, veiled in dusky shadows, was the entrance alcove to the old Brisling Department Store, a block square edifice once thriving but closed several years back: unlikely to draw the attention of passers by. Was it deep enough? Was it dark enough? A pressure at his groin told him that it must be! He set off at a fast walk and faded into the dark grotto a quarter block away, deflating at last to comfort before returning to his car.

In a similar dark hole across Goyeau Street from Brisling's entrance a lone uniformed figure leaned, whispering to his radio:

"I dunno, but I might have him. If so, he's sloppier than usual, pissing across the street like nobody sees him. Could be him. How's this sound? 'Bout five nine, ten. Could be blond: hard to tell from here. Casual slacks, leather sports jacket. How 'bout it?"

"Could be." The radio whispered back in static tones that betrayed no decision on the part of the transmittor.

It was the shadow's turn to whisper, "Should I take him?"

"Wait. We have to be sure. This is no simple arrest here. They want him out of the way. For sure! We have to make sure."

"You still got the car?"

"Yeah. You wait there. I'll wait here. If he comes to the car, we've got him. Follow the pisser when he's done."

"Right."

The uniform had only seconds to wait. Then he stepped from the shadows into the blue street light and followed. The man walked back the way he had come, toward the corner of Pitt and Goyeau, and at the corner turned. It looked as though he were walking toward the car.

Steve felt better. Urinating had cleared his bladder and the spring breeze had cleared his head. As he turned the corner by Brisling's, he paused for a moment. There, a quarter block away, was his car, a red and white 'fifty six Ford Customline hardtop. True, it was not a Crown Vicky, but it was low and sleek and a car to be proud of. In the mercury blue of the night street the rust and the dents seemed to disappear, so that the car from this distance could appear almost new. He was proud of his car. He trotted the rest of the way, leapt in and turned the key. The salt rotted muffler roared and the radio burst with American rock and roll from WLLZ. He began to pull away.

Behind the red and white Ford two shadows separated themselves from the night; two uniforms became hardened fact. One flew from around the corner, yelling to his partner, who materialised from an alcove near the back of the departing car and fell to one knee on the road. His hands rose to eye level.

Steve felt a deafening sound. In his mirror he saw a balloon burst: in slow motion a million snowflakes of glass floated toward him, drifting to rest the length of the car until, an eternity later, the final few fluttered into the windshield. In a second he realised that his rear window had vanished, disintegrated. He stopped the car. He got out. He looked up. Had some drunk dropped a bottle from the apartment across the street? He saw nobody. He looked where he had come from. Two men were running toward him. Uniforms. Police.

Almost as soon as the car moved into the streetlights, but too late to stop the shot, both policemen saw the begrimed license plates clearly: Ontario. Too late. The car had stopped.

The shooter started to stand, "Oh, God!"

His partner had caught up, "It's the wrong car! We could have wasted the wrong guy! Shit! The wrong car!"

"I think the bullet ricochetted. He could be all right. Stay cool. I'll think of something. Just stay cool!"

"But if they start checking on us..."

"I know! I know, just take my lead and I'll back away from it. You're the full constable and I'm probationary. You have to be in charge in case he knows the uniforms."

"Okay. He looks alright, but we've got to keep him from reporting...."

"Just stay cool. We'll handle it. One way or the other."

Steve stood by the back of his car.

The two men in uniform ran up to him. Only when the first spoke did it dawn on Steve that they might not have come to help, that they might indeed be the cause of his present discomfort.

"Why didn't you stop?"

"What?"

"We called for you to stop; why didn't you stop?"

"What? You, you did this?" Steve was astounded.

"You tried to get away," said the second policeman as he moved in close to Steve, standing face to face and less than a foot away, "we had no other way to stop you." The other uniform faded into the shadows at the other side of the car.

"I never saw, never heard. I was driving away, never heard you if you called..." the realisation came to him full blown, "No other way! You shot at me! You shot my window out."

"You tried to get away."

"But, why...?"

"You're drunk. We had to stop you."

"Drunk! No way! I was at the Pitt since eleven. I only had three beers..."

"That's enough."

"What?"

"Three's enough. That'll put you over the limit, legal. Besides, you were pissing in public–that's indecent exposure."

"Fuck, man! You shot at me! What is this? Since when do you kill people for urinating? That's nuts: you shot at me!"

The policeman took half a step forward. His partner remained in the shadows. Steve stepped back slightly, pointing to the cavity where his car's rear window had once been. As he moved away from the uniform's aura he could feel his anger rising. A split second later it burst from his mouth:

"You blew out my window! Look! Look at it! What are you gonna do about that? You shot at me man! What about this window? What about...?" The policeman moved forward, hovering again in a threatening manner, so that Steve stopped his tirade.

"We could find lots of charges to lay. Even if you got off, it would cost you a bundle for lawyers. But," The policeman stepped back slightly and his voice shifted from aggressiveness to a conciliatory and friendly tone, "Listen, we'll be glad to forget all the charges, forget this ever happened. After all, everyone makes a mistake sometime."

"But. You shot out my window. What about the...?"

"Like I said, everybody makes a mistake. We'll forget about the charges; you forget about the window."

The other policeman came closer, materialising from the shadows. Steve saw the emptiness of the street. He saw the two guns, now holstered but still present. He saw the shot out window. He saw the point.

"Okay."

The two uniforms said nothing. They turned and walked away, fading into the predawn darkness from which they had come. Steve got into his car and turned toward Riverside Drive.

A Gathering of Shadows   MacKenzie

Chapter Four

A block to the west and five storeys up, a solitary figure in a parked Windsor Taxi neither heard the crack of the pistol nor saw the brief drama in the street below him. Rick Bergeron was involved in a struggle of his own: with his conscience and with his curiosity. It was one thing to drive from one point to another with an envelope of money and to resist opening it. It was quite another thing to be forced to sit for a whole hour in a parked cab in an empty parking garage with a large and mysterious, obviously high priced package. The conflict was short and victory swift. For Rick, conscience mostly involved fear of getting caught and, he reasoned, if he fastened the package exactly as he had received it, no one would be the wiser. His curiosity, on the other hand, had already been piqued by the bulging brown envelope and by now was growing all out of proportion to any hold Bud and his clients might have on that frail conscience. Within fifteen minutes masking tape had been loosed, paper unfolded and corrugated flaps pulled back. For another quarter hour Rick just sat very still, looking. It took him that long to recognize, to admit to himself that he had become involved in something much bigger than a mere wine delivery service.

Rick was very careful to wrap the box exactly as before, taking the time to recall every detail. By the time he finished, the hour was almost over. Just about the same time that Steve Lansing drove up the driveway beside his small apartment, Rick Bergeron's taxi slipped out of the parking garage and drove toward University Avenue.

***

Meanwhile, on Chatham Street, a block from the Pitt Hotel and on the other side of the parking garage from the Pitt, two police constables slipped quietly into an unmarked dark blue Buick Regal. Each could see the unease in the face of the other, enhanced by the ghoulish blue cast of the Windsor street lights.

"What if he talks, Frank? What if he decides to report this? That could be real trouble!"

"Don't worry. Hey, we really scared the shit out of him! He'll keep quiet! What we've got to do is to get the yankee. Come on, let's report in and call it a night."

"Yeah, I Guess you're right. But still..."

"Listen. Don't worry. The guy'll stay cool. No problem. Let's go home." Frank started the car and pulled into Chatham Street. Dawn had still not quite come to Windsor when the blue Buick turned left on Ouellette Avenue and drove quickly away from downtown Windsor and the Detroit River.

Chapter Five

Rick's curiosity had gotten the better of him, allowed him to open the box and look inside. Now the box is closed again and sealed but in his mind it is still open, and from it the questions flow, the temptations to know more, to make the connections, to find the links between this box and his boss, between the American in the old car and the destination the box is eventually to reach, whatever that destination might be. Rick senses that he has latched onto one pot of gold, of which there may be more if only he can locate the end of some dark rainbow. His mind is weighing the risks as he rolls past the predawn buildings of University Avenue. Who is the American? How far can he question Bud? Should he let Bud know how much he has seen? The questions still flow with increasing fury from the box in his mind as he turns left into the company lot and honks his horn twice in front of the double garage door. The door opens and the blue and yellow cab rolls in.

As the door closes behind his cab Rick sees Bud coming toward him from the shadows in the back of the garage, near the dispatch office. As Rick turns off the engine and steps out of the cab, a second figure materialises from the shadows behind Bud, a man in a dark business suit, a man Rick has never seen before.

"You're late."

"He made me wait until he was gone for sure. Said there was a guy with a gun watching. I thought it better to wait."

"You got it?"

"Yeah," the questions poise at the tip of Rick's tongue but do not quite take that final leap into the dark space between him and Bud. That void is filled by the other man, who now steps forward.

"The box please."

Rick steps around the cab and takes the box from the passenger side. He walks back and, uncertain who to hand it to, holds the box toward Bud. The other man reaches over and takes it from his hands. He walks with it across the garage to a car Rick has not noticed before, one of the new small Cadillacs, black, with Michigan plates. As the man sets the box in the back seat of the Cadillac, then gets in himself, Rick unreins his growing curiosity.

"What is this, Bud? Why here? Who is this guy?"

Bud cuts off the questions in mid-leap, "Listen, Rick, you've done well. Don't spoil it by asking too many questions. And don't worry about using the garage tonight. I had Wino take over dispatch for a few hours, so everyone here is one of us. It's all okay. Now, for your own good, just lay off the questions. You did well, and I'll make sure you are well done by. You understand?"

Rick nods yes, but still the questions crowd his head, straining to be freed. The stranger is on his way toward the two men. His right hand is inside the left side of his coat, like Napoleon. He reaches Bud and whispers something. He looks concerned. Someone, possibly a chauffeur, is getting out of the black car.

Bud looks concerned too. As he moves a bit closer to Rick, he bites off the words: "The box has been opened."

Behind Bud, Rick can see the stranger slowly move his right hand out of his coat.

***

Janice jerks awake. Something has startled her, a dream perhaps, or the coolness of morning. Somehow during the night she has accidentally thrown off the covers. She is alone.

Janice checks the alarm clock: five thirty. She gets up and looks out the window, north and west toward Detroit. From Meadowbrook, far in the east end of Windsor, the skyline is just far enough away to be a ragged slash across the horizon with the new Renaissance Center the handle of the dagger responsible; already the red light of morning is oozing westward and upward along the horizon, diffusing the veil that has been laid across the sky by that massive collision of Nature with American and Canadian auto industries, Zug Island foundries, numerous support industries, and hundreds of thousands of salt-rusted exhaust systems. To Janice, the rosy pink glow of a spring morning is quite lovely. Still, Janice is worried.

Rick has not come home. It has happened before. Rick Bergeron is not always the most reliable husband. If he has to work late he might or might not call. Sometimes it was that he worked late. Sometimes something else. She never knew for sure, but he always
came home before morning. This morning is different. Where is Rick?

The other times Janice had lain awake until she heard Rick's old Torino whispering its way into the parking spot below her window, rolling in neutral to minimize the racket of the rusted muffler. She had heard the car door and then the hall door downstairs carefully opened and closed. She had pretended to sleep so that Rick could wake her if he wanted. She had always known. If he had worked late he woke her and told her. If not, he would wash up and then crawl into bed without trying to wake her; he was never in a mood for sex those nights. Some nights he didn't wash and he didn't say he worked late. She never understood that.

Janice looks again out the window and then at the clock. Where is Rick? She decides to go back to bed. She sleeps. When she wakes again, still alone, she cannot understand her dream of a sleek red and white car flowing catlike through the shadows of the Ambassador Bridge toward Detroit, its motor purring contentedly. Her own contentment has dissolved into the same thin air that has apparently consumed Rick Bergeron.

Chapter Six

Steve sits in his bay window looking out at the brightening Detroit skyline as he muses on the evening's events. The incident with the police has aroused both his anger and his curiosity. He must follow through. In a few minutes, he crosses the room to his desk, sits down and begins to type. He types ceaselessly as dawn's carmine outside his window turns to the bright white of an early spring morning. Then he addresses six envelopes.

***

Steve hopes the two policemen are off duty now. He hopes they assume he will not talk. His fingers are crossed and double crossed that his next stop will be incognito and safe. He parks several blocks from the police station and walks. As he walks in the front door he hopes the dossier type folder is inconspicuous. He asks at the main desk how to get to the office of the Chief of Police. A courteous officer behind the desk gives instructions. The route is fairly complex, so he has to ask directions several more times along the way. At the reception desk he asks for the Chief of Police. Chief Farley is in a meeting. He leaves his dossier for the Chief and exits as quickly as he can without feeling that he looks conspicuous or, worse, suspicious.

He has just left for Chief Farley a brief letter explaining the encounter with the two officers and his own subsequent fear of the police in general, along with a copy of the press release he has given all media describing the incident in detail: his method of forefending reprisals. Now he wants to be out of the building as quickly as possible. In fact, it has taken him just ten minutes from the time he parked his car to the time he arrived back from the police station. Now he feels safer. He has lodged his complaint,but he has also made sure all the local media know about the jeopardy he is in. The police will not dare act against him now.

Steve goes home.

Now that he feels safer, he thinks seriously about charging the two cops, and about suing for damages. Does he have a basis? He thinks so. He calls a few friends asking about good lawyers. He finally settles on a local civil rights expert. He does not call the lawyer. There is a problem with money. He has none.

He waits for calls about his press release. All media call and interview him on the telephone. The Star meets him beside Brisling's and takes pictures of both him and the car on location. The television station sends a crew to his apartment and interviews him in front of the car. Other calls let him know that stringers, freelance writers, have picked up the story for use in regional markets. There will be publicity throughout a two hundred mile radius.

***

"Frank, I tell you this guy's real trouble."

"What're you talking about, Les?"

"Did you see tonight's paper? Have you watched TV? Or even listened to the radio? That guy has covered the town with this story!"

"Mmmph! What?" Frank Teufel nearly chokes on his sandwich. He and his partner, Les Malenfant, have recently been meeting here at the Humble Gas Bar, a favourite truck stop near the highway, for supper before starting work. It is a chance to relax before the pressure starts. Tonight Les is not relaxed. Frank has an idea why, but since he has not checked the media, he asks, "What guy? What story?"

"The guy in the old Ford. The guy you said we scared shitless. You said not to worry. Remember?"

"So, wha'd he do?"

"Put the whole thing in the papers and on TV and everywhere, that's all!"

"All right. Cool down, Les. Listen, I'll talk to Farley, get him to shut the whole thing down if he can. Maybe the guy can't recognize us...."

"Described me!"

"Well, maybe he can be bought, or at least he'll settle for internal hearings."

"What?"

"Well, it's a possibility. If we can't squash the thing—and we can't do that except through the department now he's made it so public—we may have to stage some hearings. That way we can keep our identity hidden within the department. It's better than hitting the courts."

"It's awful risky, Frank. I don't know..."

"Listen. This job is risk. All risk! One way or the other, we will take care of it. Listen, did any of the media give this guy's name and address?"

"Yeah. He's, ah, Steve Lansing, and the TV station filmed at his place; it's upstairs from the upholstery place on Riverside."

"Good."

The two men in business suits finish their meal and leave, driving away in a dark blue Buick Regal.

Chapter Seven

"Mmn, who's that calling this early on a Saturday morning? Quiet! I'm coming! Should move phone to bedroom... Hello?"

"Good morning. Is this Mr. Steve Lansing?"

"Yeah."

"This is Staff Inspector Tarnower of the Windsor Police Department. You had placed a complaint with Chief Farley's office."

"With Chief Farley, yes." Steve is beginning to wake up.

"Can you come down to the police station today to make a formal complaint?"

"The station? But I already...."

"You left a letter. It has to be a properly filed complaint against the policemen who were involved. Can you come down today and meet with myself and Staff Sergeant Goodman to make a formal complaint?"

"Ah, yes, I suppose so. But. How early this afternoon? Say around two or three?"

"Anytime between two and three will be fine."

"Thank you."

"Oh, and bring the car. We'll have a ballistics man look at it."

"Fine, goodbye."

"Good day."

Steve makes a quick cup of coffee as he washes and dresses. The rest of the morning goes slowly for Steve. He walks to the market and picks up two steaks, top round, and some broccoli. He buys some wine, white and not too expensive, at the Bright's store on Ouellette avenue. He putters around the apartment, pretending to clean up or to work on some short stories he has begun but never finished, yet really doing very little. His mind is on a shadowed street now removed by time as well as space. He is more than a little concerned about going back into that maze of hallways that is the central police headquarters. After all, they have tried once to shoot him, and then to cover up. Have they anything to lose? Still, in broad daylight, with witnesses around....

After the morning's apprehension, the afternoon seems to go quite smoothly. The day's bright sunlight and warm spring weather have helped to ease Steve's nerves. Staff Inspector Tarnower meets him in the main lobby and leads him through a half dozen hallways to Staff Sergeant Goodman. After brief introductions and a quick apology for other pressing matters, the Staff Inspector leaves Steve with Staff Sergeant ("Call me Peter if you like.") Goodman. Peter is very kind. As he takes Steve's statement, occasionally interjecting questions or confirming specific points, he expresses concern, and even empathy, for the unease this event has caused. He says he was the Staff Sergeant on duty that night, so if any constables acted out of line he is responsible. He feels bad that Steve did not come to the police first with his story, and leave the media out. It seems to be a matter of personal pride. As he has done already in his letter to the media, Steve describes the events of last Thursday in as great detail as he can; unfortunately, because one policeman dominated the foreground while the other stood back, he can describe only one of the men with any accuracy. Peter thinks he might know who the man is. After Sergeant Goodman reads it back to him, Steve signs several copies of the statement. Peter suggests that the police department investigate the case internally and, if charges are laid, charge the men under the Police Act rather than the Criminal Code. The way he explains it, it sounds simpler both for Steve and for the police department. Either way, the culprits will be caught and punished. And Peter does seem to have everybody's best interests at heart! Steve agrees to go with charges under the Police Act. Everyone is happy.

Peter takes Steve to meet an Inspector Cordite, a man of about sixty and, by his uniform, quite a senior officer. He is the expert on ballistics. The three of them go outside to look at the car. After a brief–it seems like about five minutes– inspection of the damaged window and frame, Inspector Cordite says that it does not appear to be gunshot damage. Steve gets upset. He gains no concession from the Inspector. Peter asks the police staff to vacuum the glass out of the car. Steve realises that nobody has yet offered to pay for the damage to his car. He mentions this. Inspector Cordite suggests that the window might have broken spontaneously. Peter says he might get Steve a window cheap from his brother-in-law. Steve begins to feel the victim of some grand con game. He says goodbye and leaves. Everyone is smiling.

Saturday evening, Steve and a friend have steak dinner at his place and watch the river rolling darkly by. He spends half of Sunday on the street beside Brisling's, searching for a bullet he has not been able to locate inside his car, a bullet which may have ricochetted into the street. A man in the variety store across the street finally tells him that the streets are cleaned each morning at about four. The street has been cleaned three times since the incident. Steve goes home. Monday morning promptly at nine he calls Lionel LeBlanc, Q.C., for an appointment. Tuesday afternoon he repeats his story again, up to date. He says he has no money. The lawyer accepts the case but explains that Steve must pay disbursements as they come due. The lawyer will be paid when the suit is over. Steve agrees. He will not give up now. He will find the money when he needs it. Steve leaves the plush office of Lionel LeBlanc, Q.C., confident that he has retained the best civil rights lawyer in Windsor, perhaps Ontario, to attend to his case in the police hearings and to execute his lawsuit. He is confident. And he is happy.

Steve is without care as he drives homeward along Riverside Drive. If he cared to look, he would see behind him a dark blue Buick Regal and, at the wheel, a familiar face.

Chapter Eight

The ringing telephone slices through the dream with stiletto precision, leaving only a fine line to define where one world ends and another begins.

"Hello?"

"Is that Steve Lansing?"

"Ah, yeah. Who...?"

"I know about your problem. I saw the other car, the one they—the cops—wanted to stop. Maybe we can help each other, eh?"

"What d'you mean, help? Who are you? What do you want? What did you see?"

"Listen, I got a problem too. Maybe you can help me out and I can help you, you know. Can we get together? Tomorrow sometime?"

"Tomorrow? I guess so. Where? How will I know you?"

"How about Geno's on the river? They've got tables set up outside now, but don't sit there. Go somewhere inside, near the back. Order something. I'll come to you."

"Sounds alright. How about around two? That way the lunch rush is over. Just so I'm sure it's you, what's your name?"

"Two's good. My name is Ri..."

Ringing and ringing! The telephone is in the kitchen. Steve rolls the blankets off his still sleeping body, tumbles from the bed and stumbles in the general direction of the ringing. He is still not quite awake when he lifts the receiver.

"Hello?"

"Good morning!"

"Tracey?"

Steve has been dating Tracey Hanlon off and on for about three years now, most recently last night.

"Of course, silly. You told me to call, remember? Seven o'clock on the dot, and here I am!"

"Huh?"

"Come on. Wake up! You said you had a lot of work to do today. And after staying so late last night–well, you thought you might need some help getting up. From the sounds of you, it looks like you were right, eh?"

"Oh yeah, right, the work! Thanks for waking me and reminding me. Hey listen, did you call earlier?"

"No, why?"

"Nothing, it's just that I seem to remember another call. Something about an appointment. I must have been half asleep when I answered, or maybe I dreamed it. I dunno."

"Wasn't me."

"Well, if it's all that important, it'll come back to me. What're you doing for lunch?"

"Right now, not much."

"How about if I pick you up and we'll eat somewhere downtown?"

"Sure. About twelve thirty okay."

"Great."

"Listen, I've got to get ready for work. You get going on your work and I'll see you at noon, okay?"

"Sure, bye for now."

"Ciaou."

Steve spends the morning reviewing his research for an investigative article on organized crime in Windsor, that he hopes to write and sell. At around ten he calls Lionel LeBlanc to see how the case is going and is told that Mr. LeBlanc is in Toronto until Friday working on a governmental commission. Looking at his files, Steve can see a pattern that suggests connections, perhaps even a network, but try as he will he is unable to make the connections come together. By noon Steve finds that he has totally bogged down in the mire of paper he has collected. He welcomes the break for lunch.

During the twelve minute walk along Riverside Drive to the foot of Ouellette Avenue he continues to sift information in his mind, but he is no closer to a solution when he reaches the bank where Tracey works. Steve pauses a second in the bright spring sun, looking across Dieppe Park at the Detroit River darkly flowing between Windsor and the American city beyond. Today each ridge and rivulet sparkles with brilliant stolen portions of the sun's light. As Steve walks through the double doorway into the air conditioned fluorescent light of the bank, Tracey is just leaving her desk. Her smile is sunny as she walks toward him, passing quickly through the swinging gate in the counter and, with him, out of the bank into the brightness of midday.

"Where to."

"You invited me, Steve, why don't you decide?"

"I don't have a set lunch hour like you do. At least you should get to choose where you eat if not when."

"Okay, how about Geno's? It's just around the corner, and I think they have the tables set up in front now. It'll be nice to eat outside, where we can see the river. It's nice to be in the sun."

Steve nods his agreement and they walk westward along the riverfront. In the back of his mind, Steve senses a connection being made: a nagging feeling that he should remember something, something about Geno's Restaurant. But the memory is not complete. Tracey's voice reaches back, pulling him from the puzzle to the present.

"Oh, Steve! Look, it's full!"

Normally, on a bright, sunny day, Geno's Patio opens at twelve noon on the dot. By twelve fifteen, all the limited seating space is taken by a coterie of university students and downtown professionals. Today is no exception. Every table has been claimed by its own group of sunseekers.

"We should have known. What do you think, do you want to go somewhere else or maybe sit inside near the windows?"

"Oh, I don't know!"

"Let's go in."

"Okay, but near the window. Then we can at least look outside."

Inside the restaurant it is cool and comfortable. They choose a table at windowside and settle into the usual conversation of young people at spring: work, friends, the weather. They decide to try the noon buffet rather than the menu items. As they walk toward the back of the restaurant, where the buffet is set up, the question at the back of Steve's mind begins to nag again. The challenge of constructing a meal from the delicacies offered forces the question into temporary acquiescence. The meal is uneventful: more small talk, waves to friends passing on the street, comments on the people walking past. Only occasionally does Steve glance toward the buffet counter, a question buried deep in his eyes.

One thirty comes quickly. Tracey has an appointment at quarter to and has to leave in order to prepare the necessary papers. As they stand at the cash desk at the back of the restaurant, a telephone rings. Steve looks first at the phone behind the desk then over his shoulder to where the buffet table is just being cleared away. A shock of memory has just registered on his face.

"Sir? Sir, your change!" It is the girl behind the cash register reaching out to him with a handful of coins and a few bills.

"Huh?" Steve jerks back to reality, "Oh yeah, thanks."

"Steve? What's wrong?"

"Ah, nothing. Why?"

"You looked funny just now, and you seemed kind of lost, you know?"

"It's nothing important. I just remembered an appointment I made. Listen, Tracey, do you mind going back to the bank on your own? I'd like to hang around here for a while."

"What?"

"That other phone call this morning, I remember what it was. A guy wants to meet me here at two. Says he knows something about the shooting. I just want to wait and see if he shows."

"I thought you said you dreamed the call."

"Maybe dreamed. Maybe not. I just want to check it out."

"Steve... well, okay."

"Thanks, Trace. I just want to be sure. I'll see you later." He kisses her quickly on the forehead. She walks out the door into the

24

sunshine and back to the bank. Steve sits at a table in the back and orders a beer. He tries to remember the caller's name. He cannot. He waits.

Chapter Nine

At about the same time, two men in dark business suits are being shown by a secretary into the office of Robert Farley, Chief of Police.

"Well, gentlemen, how can I help you?"

There is a pause as the secretary exits and closes the door behind, then one of the two walks to the Chief's desk, laying down a small handful of documents.

"These should serve to identify us. My name is Frank and Les here is my partner. If you need any further confirmation of who we are, there is a telephone number and name on the top paper."

The Police Chief riffs quickly through the half dozen papers, each in its turn receiving his cursory glance. He looks up at his two visitors, then pauses before speaking.

"Please have a seat gentlemen. Of course, I had some idea who you were or you would never have gotten to see me so quickly–still, if you don't mind, I think I will make that call. Just to confirm for certain, you know."

The two settle into the plush armchairs across from the Chief's desk and wait quietly while he makes the call.

"Hello. This is Robert Farley, Chief of Police for the City of Windsor. Who am I speaking to please? Ah, Sergeant Groves, good morning. Have you a Commander Pazitch there? Good. May I speak to him please?"

After a pause of thirty seconds or so, which seems to the Chief interminable, he resumes the conversation.

"Commander Pazitch? Yes, ah, this is Chief Farley at the Windsor Police Department. I have two men here who say they work for you, or at least that you can confirm their identities.... Yes, that's right, Frank and Les. Sir, have they been working in Windsor long?" Consternation clouds his face as he hears the long distance answer, and it brings a bite to his voice when, after a pause, he speaks again.

"We should have known! Should have been told! A year, that's a long time! And we were never told! Why? What...?"

Another pause.

"But..."

A much longer pause, as the Chief's normally ruddy face grows redder then almost blue with the emotion he is obviously having trouble controlling.

"But I still think... Yes sir. Thank you sir. I'll take care of it Commander. Good day sir."

He sits for a moment, his grim face broadcasting a turmoil of pent-up emotions, then he hangs up the telephone and presses the button on his desktop intercom.

"Miss Davis, I do not want to be disturbed. By anyone!"

As soon as his secretary's confirmation comes from the box on his desk, the Chief turns, ashen faced, to the two interlopers, speaking in subdued but not convivial tones.

"Okay, I don't like it one bit, but it looks like I'm obligated to help you. Now what's it all about?"

"You've had some problems, bad press and so on, recently. Apparently two of your constables took a shot at someone. We thought Les and I could help you take care of it."

"So that's it. I suspected as much. What do you need from me?"

"You'll have to find the constables involved, suspend them, have hearings. I understand this guy Lansing has agreed to internal prosecution; that's good. Get the hearings through smoothly and everything should be okay. Do you have someone who can handle it—reliable people?"

"Reliable?"

"Yes, people on your staff you can trust to handle the hearings discreetly. And not ask questions."

"I'll take care of it."

"Good." Frank is getting up from his chair and walking to the desk, a new bundle of papers in his hand; he sets it down and picks up the bunch earlier laid down as identification. "We have seen the complaint Lansing filed. These papers will give you names for the constables and the specific charges to be laid. He seems to have a good memory for faces, judging by the media reports and the complaint, so we will be available for the hearings too."

"How will I contact you if I need you?"

"You won't. We will contact you. As far as you are concerned, you still don't even know we're in town."

"Just tell me, what's this all about?"

"It has nothing to do with you. Remember, as far as you are concerned this is simply a matter of disciplining a couple of your policemen who have gotten out of line. Nothing more. You've spoken with the Commander. That's all you need to know."

"All right. I still don't like it, but if it has to be that way...."

"It does. We'll be going now. Please get things moving as quickly as possible."

Silence fills the office of the Chief of Police as the second visitor rises and both move across the room and out the door, closing it quietly behind them. Robert Farley sits reading, the already clouded expression on his face growing blacker and blacker. After ten minutes or so, he speaks into the plastic box on his desk.

"Miss Davis."

"Yes sir?"

"Staff Sergeant Goodman should be in the building somewhere. Can you please locate him. I want to see him, here, right away."

"Yes sir."

"And when you're done that, can you please find Inspector Tarnower and Inspector Renaud. I'll want to see them immediately after I am done with Sergeant Goodman. If they are out of the building, have them come in and stand by."

"Yes sir."

Chapter Ten

Steve is still sitting at the back of a nearly empty restaurant, still waiting for a man who may have been a dream. He looks at his watch: three twenty. He finishes his beer, the third, and gets up to leave.

As he is walking past the still thronging tables outside Geno's, preoccupied with the circumstances surrounding the broken appointment and the events of the past week or so, his own name breaks his reverie, coming to him mysteriously and without direction in much the same way that sudden sunshine will sometimes burn through a cloudy day. He stops.

Looking around he sees, seated at one of the outdoor tables in the shade of the building, a group of friends and acquaintances. The young woman who has just called and is now beckoning cheerfully is Jane Lesley, a freelance columnist for several publications and sometimes editor for The Windsorite, a local entertainment magazine. She is about twenty five, slender, blonde, and quite pretty. Steve knows Jane through having submitted articles to her from time to time. The others he knows socially, through parties and chance meetings such as this one.

Trixie LaBelle, who is next to Jane at the table, is a divorced mother of two, in her mid-thirties, a handsome brunette with a modishly short haircut and tasteful clothing. While she aspires to be an actress and has played some cast of thousands roles in Toronto movies, her unique name derives not from show business but from a childhood nickname and the legacy of her former husband, Harry

LaBelle. While at this time Trixie looks quite demure, Steve recalls that the first time he met her, again with Jane Lesley, she had insisted on going to The Palace, a local bar featuring strippers, and auditioning. In fact, Trixie never got beyond discussing rates of pay and the best times to audition. Her actual performance was not so much postponed as prorogued with diplomatic showmanship. Trixie enjoys creating an impression.

Bill Monaghan is a foreman at the main Chrysler Corporation plant on Tecumseh Road, a solid Windsor union man proud to work at "Chrysler's," and equally proud of his ability to party. He is a handsome man in his late thirties, divorced and supporting three children.

Brian Donovan is a thirtyish black man, never married and at present unemployed. He has been known to work from time to time, driving a cab or acting as doorman at a couple of bars, but for the most part he seems to just drift from party to party. Although he is unemployed, he always seems to have the money for stylish clothes and for pot and liquor. He is a very convivial fellow.

The third man, who is introduced as Mark Ledlow, a twenty three year old reporter for The Star , has been at many of the same parties as Steve but this is the first time the two have actually met.

Steve joins the party at the table. While the conversation moves through several subjects, melding easily from one to the other and eventually back again, inevitably Steve's adventure comes to the fore.

"Hey, you're getting to be quite famous. In the papers, on TV, every place I look, there's Steve Lansing. You don't seriously mean to go through with this, do you?"

"I have to, Jane. Listen, they shot at me and then tried to cover it up. Do you realize what a mess our world will be if we let the police get away with that? They're supposed to protect us, not rule or bully us!"

"That's like playing Don Quixote; you can't joust with the police department. You can get hurt."

"That's why I took it to the media. I figure that now if anything happens to me, people will know who did it—so nothing will happen."

"I don't know," Bill is speaking, "I hear a lot of stuff around the plant. Guys get blasted. The cops pound the shit out of 'em just for the hell of it. If they complain, the cops haul them in on some false charges and do it again. Then they release them, saying maybe the guy they wanted had the same name only spelled different, something like that. Happens all the time."

Young Mark Ledlow is looking perplexed, "That's only hearsay. A bunch of factory workers making idle gossip to fill the time. If it happens so much, how come we don't see more of it in the media? How come we don't have investigations like in Kitchener or Toronto?"

Mark's words transport Steve to a friend's story about a month ago. A thirtyish working class type had come in. He had been to his lawyer's about suing the city police. According to him, the police had arrested him at his house, taken him to the station, and beaten him for several hours. They laid no charges and finally released him, saying that they had thought him to be Doug McPherson, whereas he was Doug MacPherson, spelling his name with the slight but obvious difference of "Mac."

Steve also remembers some of the homosexuals at the Pitt Hotel speaking of police harassment and of random beatings, but he had always thought these stories to be apocryphal subculture paranoia, not to be taken at all seriously.

In searching through newspapers for information, he has occasionally seen similar stories. One in particular he remembers had shocked him. A man claimed that he went inside the police station to complain about a parking ticket he had been issued, and that three policemen had taken him into a back room and had thoroughly beaten him. At the time Steve had thought there must be more to it than that; now he is not so sure.

He is carried back to the group around the table by the sound of Trixie's voice.

"...and Harry used to have several friends on the police. Some of them used to brag about who they beat up. A couple of them even the other cops are afraid of. And there's one, a good friend so I won't say his name, but one day Harry came home really shocked: something about this guy, but he wouldn't say what. Well, finally a few weeks later, I got it out of him: it seems this policeman, who we all thought was so straight, was using his badge to get girls. He'd go into a bar and threaten to charge them with prostitution unless they went to bed with him. Harry actually saw him do it. I wouldn't go against them. Not for anything. The bad ones have too much power, and they cover up for each other. You can't win!"

"I agree," Brian Donovan says, "No matter what you do or how much you may think you've won, they'll get you in the end. They beat on you if you're black. They beat on the queers. They beat on the   poor old winos. They just do it and they're not about to stop for one man. Man, I've seen 'em get to a lot of my friends but, much as I don't like it, I know there's nothing I can do. Like Trix says, they're just too well organized. Most of the cops are good, but those few bad guys play so rough and cover up so well for each other that the good cops won't mess in...."

The conversation continues in the same vein until about seven thirty, combining social news, the silliness which comes with successive beers in the heat of spring, and concern over the jeopardy into which Steve has flung himself. At some point, several people express their disappointment at having seen Steve pass them by in his car without so much as a wave or a honk of his horn. On thinking back to the several occasions they mention, Steve thinks that he was either at other areas of the city or not in his car at all. He wonders if his friends have perhaps confused their dates or times.

When the air cools and the breeze from Detroit starts cutting through summery daytime clothing, the group at the table disperses homeward. Steve enjoys the leisurely walk along Riverside Drive to his apartment. He still has a few hours left for research this evening if the walk can overcome the relaxing effect of the beer. If not, there is always television.

Although beginning to take on some of the paranoia of his erstwhile companions, Steve has not yet begun to keep to the shadows or to peer nervously over his shoulders. He does not, as he opens the door to the lower landing of his apartment, notice the dark blue car parked in the railway freight yard across the drive.

Chapter Eleven

"Don't worry, Steve. It's all going well, quite quickly in fact. Once we get these hearings over, we'll commence with the lawsuit. The evidence supports our side, so the action should proceed smoothly against Porter and Butler."

"You don't see any difficulty? You're sure I haven't made a mistake in letting them prosecute this through the department? Sometimes I feel like I'm part of a huge con game. I mean with this setup, I'm not even the one laying the charges anymore. I've become just a witness for the prosecution, and the prosecution is cops against cops; are you sure they'll be honest about it?"

"Steve, don't worry. You've had one bad experience, that's all. The hearing is public, and I'll be right there with you to observe what happens. Even with a motive for falsifying or covering up, there will be no opportunity. Just go home. Relax. I'll see you here Wednesday around nine thirty, okay?"

Steve leaves Lionel LeBlanc's plush office with a ripe kernel of doubt still plumping in his mind. He is not at all certain that he can excise it by the time of the first hearing. In the four weeks since his name and address first hit the media he has often noticed police cars following him as he drives around the city. He has also noticed a rainbow of LTD's: red, brown, green, blue, beige—the fleet of city detectives, as he has come to recognize them. They do nothing. He drives with care. Still, it worries him. Are they attempting to intimidate him? Why? He has brought the charges; isn't it too late? And sometimes, more often than any specific one of the other cars in fact, he sees the Buick, dark blue and following.

Friends who feel the need to know these things have told Steve that the O.P.P. and R.C.M.P. cars are numbered sequentially because the plates are all bought at the same time, and they have told him the numbers to check for. The plates on the Buick do not fit either set. Steve figures that the Windsor Police must have Buicks as well as Fords for their detectives. Other than that, he has no real reason to worry.

He now knows the names of his assailants: Constable Lester Butler and Constable Frank Porter. He knows that one has two years experience on the force and should have known better, and he thinks it a shame that the other is only probationary, drawn into a bad situation by his partner. He is not happy with the charges under the Police Act, something to do with misapplication of duty or with being in the wrong place at the wrong time rather than dealing more specifically with the shooting, but apparently these are the most appropriate, and, whatever the charges, the shooting is the crux. Peter Goodman says that the two claim that Butler only threw a rather heavy non-regulation flashlight at the car, and that the impact of the light broke the window. This too, seems all right to Steve. After all, who would believe such a story: that a flashlight thrown some thirty or forty feet could have such an impact!

Yet Steve's unease grows.

***

The first hearing runs as smoothly as a bit of well staged theatre, something by Beckett perhaps, running from ten o'clock Wednesday morning until about three in the afternoon with a half hour break for lunch. The cast of characters is small: Staff Inspector John Tarnower, counsellor for the prosecution; Staff Inspector Serge Renaud, counsellor for the defence; the accused, Constable Lester Butler and Probationary Constable Frank Porter; Stephen Lansing, witness for the prosecution; Staff Sergeant Peter Goodman, witness for the prosecution; Inspector Raymond Cordite, witness for the defence; Andrew Hackett, taxi driver, witness for the defence; and Departmental Inspector Solomon Urizen, presiding officer for the hearing on behalf of the City of Windsor Police Department. With the exception of Stephen Lansing, who is the first witness, all witnesses are kept in an anteroom until it is their turn to testify. Steve remains in the hearing for the duration.

As Steve sees it, all goes well for his side. He tells the story again as he has done so many times before. Staff Sergeant Goodman tells that the two have admitted stopping Steve's car but that they claim not to have shot, rather to have thrown a flashlight. He exhibits a sample, which he says was taken from Butler's locker. It is very heavy, and the front of it is bent. Steve still doubts that it could have been thrown as far or as fast as claimed. The taxi driver was in the area but did not see much of anything. He testifies that he saw two policemen talking to another man beside a stopped, older car. He cannot recall what any of the men looked like. Inspector Cordite says that the damage on the flashlight is consistent with the damage at the base of Steve's rear window frame. He says that no bullet was ever found. Pressured, he admits little if any effort was put into looking for the bullet.

During Steve's testimony, Staff Inspector Renaud has accused him of making the whole story up, of seeking publicity, has generally badgered him. During the break he is friendly, treats it as a game, apologises for his actions, tells Steve it all means nothing, that there is nothing personal in it, and that he in fact sympathises with Steve but is just doing his job.

After the break, the two accused testify. Their stories disagree on several major points. It starts to sound as if Porter is trying to cover up for Butler but is nervous about doing so. Parts of their story seem memorized, almost as though they had discussed exact wordings together. Much of Porter's testimony seems more to corroborate Steve's than that of his partner. Asked to identify the two, Steve recalls Butler quite clearly but cannot be positive about Porter. Inspector Urizen asks a few questions of his own then closes the hearing, saying that all parties concerned will receive a copy of his report. The next day, Lionel LeBlanc's office receives the confirmation that Constable Butler has been found to be at fault. The hearing on Constable Porter is scheduled for the following Friday. Steve is happy to hear the news. It all seems almost too easy.

Chapter Twelve

The sun has only begun to rise on Monday morning as the ringing of the telephone pulls Steve from his comfortable bed to the cool linoleum of the kitchen. He is not quite awake as he picks up the receiver.

"Hello."

"You Steve Lansing?"

"Yes?"

"I saw an item in Saturday's paper about your problem with the cops. Are you really satisfied with that, that coverup!?"

"Who are you?"

"Someone who knows. There's more to it than just what they're doing down at the cop shop. I know. I know a lot of stuff." "What do you want? Why are you calling?"

"Maybe I don't like what's happening. Maybe I need some help from you and I want to trade. Maybe I just need to talk about it."

"What help? How could I possibly help you? Who are you, anyway?"

"Just call me Wino. Listen, if I talk, they'll find out. I'll have to skip–fast! They're everywhere, even in the cops, eh! I don't know who to talk to, but I figure you're safe, so long as we meet quick and quiet. If I can get to T.O., I'll be alright. I got friends that will take care of me there, get me to my next stop. If I tell you, maybe you or that chick, Tracey, can get me to T.O.; you know, drive up."

"Tracey? How do you know about Tracey? That wasn't in any of the stories. Nowhere. She's just a friend."

"I told you, I know lots. Do we meet?"

"I don't know, I..."

"Listen. I got your number. It's not listed, right. I know about your chick. I can tell you more; there was another car, sort of like yours, and a cabbie, Rick Bergeron, and—well, let's talk when we meet."

Steve's curiosity is aroused. He has wondered about another car, a mysteriously vanished doppelganger to his own, which could have partially caused his current shifts in lifestyle. And there is that name: Rick Bergeron. He has heard it before, in a dream perhaps, or met the man in passing. He is not sure.

"Okay. Where? When?"

"How about Geno's? Inside, near the back. Around two. It's near your place and it's pretty private that time of day. Alright?"

"Uh, okay, Geno's at two. it's Wino, right? How will I know you?"

"Just be there. I'll find you."

The telephone clicks off the line without a goodbye. Steve is feeling disoriented, perhaps partially because of being awakened so abruptly and so early, but also because of a growing sense of deja vu, partial recall of another early morning call, of another appointment made but never met. For the rest of the morning, Steve works on his research and attempts some of the writing he has not been doing for the past month. He does not accomplish much in either endeavour.

The day has turned out to be typical for Windsor in spring, humid and hazy, and Steve's distraction over the pending appointment has left his mind as hazy and his thoughts as diffused as the glowing sun outside his window. By noon he is simply marking time, waiting for two o'clock and his appointment with a voice named Wino.

***

By two o'clock most of the lunch hour crowd has cleared out of Geno's and back to downtown offices and banks, leaving the interior almost empty and the outside tables filled with unemployed university students and would-be intellectuals of various sorts. From the shade at the back of the deserted restaurant the brightly lit sunseekers, framed as they are by the large plate glass windows, seem to Steve almost to become the vast human panorama of an Italian film, civilization set against the hazy blue sky above Detroit's slums and factories. He has nearly finished one beer and is beginning to think in Bertolucci images. His mood anticipates the revelation he is sure must come shortly.

Half an hour and another beer later, Bergman black and white seems more appropriate as he looks around the nearly empty room, sensing the desolation of the modern age.

At three o'clock, he rises and walks back into the hazy brilliance of the afternoon sunshine, his eyes blinking in sudden adjustment and his mind rejecting the romance of cinema for, for nothing perhaps but a sense of being caught up in a repetitious dream he is unable to control. His body is beginning to celebrate the recently finished fourth bottle of beer as he turns up Ouellette Avenue, away from the river and toward the Shenendoah Hotel. At five, he is still sitting in the dark of the Shenendoah, drinking beer and watching a young blonde as she sheds layers of diaphanous pink until only she is left.

He will do no more work today.

Chapter Thirteen

Almost everyone who attended the first hearing is present for the second, the only exception being Andrew Hackett, the taxi driver, who has not been called to testify again. For Steve, the past week has been oblivion, passing almost as though there has been no interim from one hearing to the next. When he was not lost in the nether world of his newspaper clippings and notes he has spent his time in the day-long dusk and night-long dinginess of several downtown bars. With the exception of his second failed appointment at Geno's, the week has been quite uneventful for Steve.

Now he is sitting through another round of testimony that seems identical to that given at the first hearing, spoken by the same people in the same air conditioned boardroom. The only changes are that the two accused seem to have even less accord between their respective tales and that Steve, while he was quite ready to identify the man known as Butler, is not absolutely certain of the man who is called Porter, the man who was mostly in the shade on the night in question. The defence counsel, Staff Inspector Renaud, seizes on this inability to definitely accuse his client, but Staff Inspector Tarnower points out that Porter was with Butler on that night and has admitted to stopping Steve: The issue is not who stopped him as much as how and why.

At one point, Steve also mentions that he has seen police cars, both marked and unmarked, following him. All three inspectors express doubt that this is happening. Perhaps it is just that police cars, in their normal duties, happen to be on the same road as is

Steve? Or, if in fact Steve is being followed, the men involved are doing it of their own volition and not under departmental orders? At any rate, Departmental Inspector Urizen says that he will have it checked into and, if it is in fact happening, will have it stopped. This time, because much of the information is repetitious and there is much less reexamination of witnesses, the hearing takes only about two and a half hours, adjourning shortly after twelve-thirty. Departmental Inspector Urizen says he will have a written draft of his decision by Monday, with typed copies to everyone concerned by Tuesday morning. Lionel LeBlanc, Q.C., is confident what the decision will be.

***

Steve is seated in the posh offices of his lawyer on the twenty fifth floor of the Maple Leaf Building, an edifice of concrete and copper coated glass in downtown Windsor. Lionel LeBlanc has just told him the hearings have found in his favour. Both policemen involved are very likely to be transferred and very unlikely ever to see a promotion in rank. Steve feels badly about this in a sense: that such a singular error can lead to such long lived consequences. On the other hand, he is happy—even proud—to have stood up for his rights, indeed to have stood up for the rights of all citizens everywhere. His lawyer wakes him from his reverie by reminding him that it is not all over yet. Now they must consider the lawsuit: payment for damage to Steve's car and for the legal fees. The mechanics of this action will affect Steve only peripherally, since it is a procedure of legalities and negotiation which must, for the most part, be performed by the attorneys for the two parties involved. Lionel LeBlanc thinks it is possible he can get a settlement out of court, saving both time and fees. He will start with a claim for four thousand dollars and hope eventually to get about half that amount. He explains to Steve that much of this procedure has more to do with barter than with rightness, but that Steve has the upper hand.
Now Steve must wait.

Chapter Fourteen

Janice Bergeron is waiting to hear the worst. She is not just worried; she is distraught. It has been more than a month and Rick, her husband, has not returned to their Meadowbrook Lane townhouse. She has reported this to the city police but they can promise nothing, cannot offer the smallest glimmer of hope.

And Janice Bergeron is dreaming: big bright Technicolor dreams set in some sort of mystical world just beyond Windsor. The dreams drive Janice not just to distraction but to dread. She has had these dreams, or dreams a lot like them, before.

***

As a six year old child, little Janice Smith had once dreamed of a visit from her Uncle Barney, who lived more than a thousand miles away. It seemed real to the child. Uncle Barney had come right into her bedroom by way of the window and had sat on the side of her bed, looking down and smiling at her. He had spoken to her but even the same night she could not recall what he had said. She had walked with him back to the window where, with one final look back, he had floated over the sill and into the starlit sky, dissolving as he went into a mist of coloured lights and nothingness. Little Janice had thought this was a very good trick and had laughed very hard, hard enough to wake her mother in the next bedroom, who had come in and found her laughing by the bedroom window, and had put her back to bed.

The next morning, Mrs Smith had sat with her daughter and tried to explain death in childlike terms; her brother Bjorn, the child's uncle, had passed away during the night.

Janice had had other dreams like that, dreams where she saw people she knew, or sometimes did not know but would subsequently meet, or sometimes her own pets, and what she saw in her dreams seemed to happen in slightly less figurative form in real life. Although convinced of her own clairvoyance, Janice gradually stopped having the dreams as she approached the age of twelve.

***

Now, at twenty eight, she is dreaming nearly every night. Every night the dream changes, sometimes slightly and sometimes almost totally, almost like some sort of nocturnal soap opera. Janice feels like Madame Sosostris, holding up the cards and waiting for her predictions to come real; yet Janice does not really understand the dreams or what they might mean, except that they fill her entire soul with foreboding. Each day Janice goes through the same routines she has followed for the five years she and Rick Bergeron have been married. She tidies up the house. She goes to her promotional job at Ford's, as the locals call the Windsor Plant of the Ford Motor Company. She returns home to read or to watch television. On the weekend she stays in. Her marriage has reached the point that Rick's absence is hardly noticed. He has long been in the habit of leaving early for work and arriving home late at night. He and she had lately seemed only to meet in bed and in the hallway outside the bathroom, passing each other with the greeting grunts of strangers, or passing in silence. It is not so much that Janice cares anymore about Rick or what has happened to him as that she imagines she has seen it, and she wants to be sure.

Until she is certain of Rick's whereabouts, of his fate, she cannot be free to continue with her own life. Besides, Janice knows from experience that her dreams, if they are in fact representations of actual events, will not end until their prophesies have come to pass.

Janice is waiting for the dreams to end.

Chapter Fifteen

The morning haze is lifting from the water and a hole is being burned in its delicate lace by a yellow globe above. Janice is walking along the shoreline. She is not sure, but she thinks she is waiting for someone. She hears in the distance the sound of a great cat purring and is suddenly aware that the dawn has turned to dusk, a deep red gash along the water with the mist glowing white above it and the sun burning red at the centre of everything. In the haze that great red ball distorts and becomes shaped almost like the head of the great cat she still hears purring not so far away. She stops and stares at its centre, entranced by its brilliance and nearness.

Out of the fiery globe, apparently walking on the surface of the water, emerges the form of a man. She is not certain, but she thinks he is the same man she has seen driving a car in her dreams. He is halfway between the sun and the beach where she stands. Now she can see the vague outline of a boat wrapped about his feet in the mist.

He seems to be beckoning or holding something or both. Now he is only a few yards from her and she can see that he is the driver of the car. He is beckoning her with his left hand to come toward him. She will not. She fears the fire that has followed him across the water and is now licking at his back. He sets down what he has been holding in his right hand, a fairly large box with what looks like a rope carrying handle. As he opens it a brilliant rainbow rushes out. Just as quickly the rainbow becomes Rick, who also beckons.

43

As she starts to step forward, both figures dissolve, becoming ever more pastel lights upon the mist. As she turns to go on with her walk, she senses that the sand of the shore has turned to concrete.

The purring is still there, filling her world, and as she turns around trying to discover the source of the sound she discovers she is not alone: opposite her on the paved road that she now perceives herself to have been walking is the red and white car. This time it is different somehow and she looks closer to see why, then it dawns on her that the sparkling chrome strip across the roof is gone. The driver gets out and starts to walk toward her. She sees that it is not the driver but the other man, the man who looks like the driver but chases the car on foot. As he approaches he holds his hand toward her and she reaches out to take it.

As their hands touch, they each sense that they are now standing on the bridge, that the ends are dissolving in the fog, making their small section rapidly shorter. Next to them is the car with the chrome strip returned to its roof. As they look on, the car becomes one with the mists around it, vanishing totally in only seconds. All that is left is the diminishing bridge that she and the stranger stand on. The man has been talking to her but the only word she has heard was "Wino." She does not understand.

Janice and the stranger are standing on a small section of bridge in the haze of morning. The haze seems to be eating the bridge from around and under them until there must soon be nothing left but morning mist and two people falling: Janice and another falling, falling, falling....

Her eyes ease open in the bright morning sun that floods her room with whiteness as the ringing of the telephone brings Janice quickly back to the real world around her and she stumbles across the room after her robe.

Chapter Sixteen

"Good morning, is Mr. Bergeron there?"

"Rick?"

"Yes, Rick Bergeron. Is he at home?"

"No, he's not."

"Do you know when he'll be back? It's very important that I talk to him."

"No. I have no idea when he'll be here. Who is this, please?"

"My name is Steve, Steve Lansing...ah, is this Mrs. Bergeron?"

"Yes, it is."

"Perhaps you can help me then, Mrs. Bergeron. There is something that has been bothering me for a while now and I thought...."

"Wait a minute! Who are you? Why are you calling here? How do you know Rick? Who are you anyway?"

"I ah, I don't actually know your husband, Mrs. Bergeron, only his name and that he works for Windsor Cabs. I called there and they said he hadn't worked for quite a while. There's a lot of Bergerons in the book but the guy I talked to at the taxi company told me you live on Meadowbrook. I looked you up in the book, and I called you because...well, I wanted to talk to your husband, ask him some questions."

"Questions? What questions?" Janice has learned to be suspicious when strangers call for Rick, especially strangers who have questions to ask; she wonders what he has been up to this time.

"Who do you work for Mr., Mr. Lansing?"

"No, I don't think you understand. You see, I'm calling on my own. I think your husband may have called me about a month or so ago and tried to see me. I may have dreamed it, but I thought he called and made an appointment to see me. He never showed up, and...."

"You may have dreamed it?"

"Yes, it was very early in the morning, eh. I almost forgot about the call and missed the appointment myself, and I wasn't even quite sure about the name until the other call came."

"What other call? Who are you anyway? Is this Rick's idea of a joke? For your information, if you don't already know, Rick took off over a month ago! I haven't seen him since! Why don't you go bother someone else?"

"Hey! Listen, I'm serious. I did get that call. And the second one too! That's what made me so sure I didn't dream the first one, and now that I've found there is a Rick Bergeron who drives cabs, I'm even more sure! Listen, if he's gone can I at least talk to you about it?"

"About what? Some dream telephone call?"

"No, not that. I had some problems with the police. Their fault, not mine. When he called, he said he might know something. The other guy that called said he knew about Rick, and something about the cab company, and about my problem with the cops too. He also made an appointment but never showed. Hey, listen, maybe you know him, eh. Maybe he was a friend of Rick's? He just gave a nickname, 'Wino'. Do you know him?"

"Wino?"

"Yeah. Do you know him?"

"No. But I think I would like to meet with you anyway. I have a few questions of my own."

"Okay, I live downtown. Do you want to meet down here or out at your end of town somewhere?"

"Let's meet downtown, say sometime this afternoon."

"Okay. How about Geno's. It's pretty convenient, only...my two no-show appointments were for inside, so let's meet outside on the patio. It's a nice sunny day anyway. Say around three?"

"Sure. I'll see you at three."

46

"What do you look like? How will I recognize you?"
"I have a feeling I will know you. Don't worry. I'll find you."

***

At five to three, Janice Bergeron parks her car at Dieppe Gardens on the riverfront below the block of buildings which includes Geno's Restaurant. All day she has been playing with the name "Wino", turning it and toying with it, trying to decipher the name that has moved out of her dream world and into the real. She is distracted, no, abstracted into her own mind as she steps out of her Vega and walks across the parking lot toward the stairs to Riverside Drive.

As she walks, she wonders if she was not too hasty in not asking for a description of her caller. After all, the coincidence of the name might be only that, a coincidence. The Wino in her dream might not be the Wino of the telephone call. Her doubts are somewhat allayed as a spark of sunlight catches her peripheral vision and she turns toward the bright reflected light. There, before her eyes in every detail, is the car that has been haunting her dreams every night. Only in one detail is it different, there is no sparkling chrome bar across the roof. As she hesitates then steps toward the car, she sees that there is another difference: in place of a rear window this old car has a sheet of clear plastic attached with masking tape. She walks along the driver's side of the car, across the back between the trunk and the hillside, and along the passenger's side, peering in the windows as she carries out her circuit. The inside is the same too. The broken back window triggers a recollection; she thinks she remembers seeing something on television, or perhaps in the paper, about a car like this having its window broken. Perhaps that's the trouble with police her caller mentioned. Perhaps this is the gate through which the car moved into her dreams: nothing mystical at all.

At the top of the hill she pauses for a few seconds to check the crowd that threatens to overflow the outdoor patio area. There, alone at a corner table, is a blond man in his late twenties. He looks very much like the man in her dreams.

47

She decides to try him and see. She walks across the pavement of Riverside Drive and approaches the table. As she does so, he rises, extending his right hand as he speaks her name. She extends her hand in return, then they both sit at the table in the hot afternoon sun.

Chapter Seventeen

It is nearly three weeks since the second hearing at the city police station, a week to the day since Frank Teufel had handed a cheque for slightly more than twenty two hundred dollars to the Chief of Police and the City of Windsor had in turn issued a cheque in the identical amount to Steve Lansing.

At the Humble Gas Bar, two men in business suits order coffee, no food. Once the order is delivered, one leans slightly across the table toward the other.

"I still don't like it, Frank. I tell you it hasn't worked!"

"I know. I figured if he saw us, identified us...well, if the hearings went smoothly and he picked up a few bucks besides, that then he would let it drop. What's wrong with him anyway?"

"And Frank, a lot of people have seen us. Everyone at the hearings knows us."

"No they don't. They know Butler and Porter, two uniformed cops. One uniform looks the same as another. Even the chief doesn't know exactly who we are or what we are doing here. Even he doesn't know our correct names. And the cops think it's all over. There's no worry there."

"But, Lansing?"

"Yes, Lansing. What are we going to do about Mr. Steve Lansing?"

"Frank, he's going to get in the way. We have to do something soon. Before he gets hurt; before he gets us hurt."

"Even more important, Les: we have to find out more about him. He may not be all he seems—or he may be more."

49

"What do you mean? He's a bum, a would be writer. He just happened to be in the wrong place at the wrong time, that's all. He just lucked into our way. What more could we possibly need to know?"

"Think of it. Here he is. He looks like the yankee. He drives a car that's almost exactly the same as the yankee's. He shows up at just about the exact time and place we expect to catch the yankee. Does that sound like coincidence?"

"Well, I don't..."

"And if he's just after vindication for a simple mistake by the police, why is he still pushing the issue? He's got his fucking convictions. He's got a good bit of money. What's he really after?"

"Who cares? We know he's still nosing around, calling that taxi company, hanging around those queer bars and the strip places too. And talking to all kinds of people, asking questions. We don't need to know about him. We just need to shut him up!"

"How do you suggest? Permanent?"

"There must be a way, Frank."

"I can't think of any other way right now. Let's find out more about him first. Let's see what his motives really are. Let's see if there is anybody else behind him. Shutting him up may not be enough if there is anybody else involved."

"I guess you're right, Frank, but I still think we should keep a very close watch on him at least. We can't afford him discovering too much."

"He won't. He's off on an entirely wrong trail."

"I wish we could be sure."

Both men lapse into thoughtful silence. Finishing their coffee plus a second cup each as the grey of dusk slips smoothly into the darker garb of night, they then rise slowly, pay their bill and return to the Buick. Each man, in the solitary chamber of his own thoughts, realizes that he has through some accident of fate been bound, perhaps irrevocably, for better or worse, to the life and movements of the failed young writer, Steve Lansing. Each is mulling, weighing and balancing the various ways this bond might be broken, sorting and sifting which might work with ease and which might recoil and cause more harm than would be done by leaving the bond intact.

Chapter Eighteen

Outside, the summer streets are scorching with the three o'clock sunshine, seething with southern Ontario humidity, and blinding with the concrete reflected brightness that keeps even American tourists indoors for the bulk of the afternoon.

Only occasionally does this sun reach a ray into the dingy false night at the Shenendoah Tavern at the corner of Ouellette and Wyandotte. The doors that swing with the regular entrances and exits of businessmen and bikers, welfare recipients and out of work auto workers do not admit the sun. Between the doors and the room where the dancers perform, there is a right angled staircase, a lobby, a swinging door: a whole maze that none but the most crooked, diffuse and indirect beam of light could ever penetrate. Here the light is the blue, the red, the green of the lights the girls splash across their own swaying forms as they perform the daily ritual for their carnal audience. Only once in a while, when one of their audience lifts a slat of the oversized venetian blind type window coverings to look out, perhaps for an expected friend or for a taxi, does the sun seize the opportunity to bathe the room in white. The intrusion from outside is gone as quickly as it comes, but the practiced observer, the reporter with a rapid eye, can discover what this room once was, and what it has become over the past thirty years or so.

Steve is at his usual table by the wall opposite the window. He has the back of his chair leaned against the wall and his feet are up on another of the four chairs at his table. He is quite relaxed. He knows the dancers by name. He knows a few of the other regular customers. He knows that no one will bother him here. The interruptions are few: a fellow customer asking to share the table if the room is full, Marj asking if he wants another beer, occasionally someone trying to sell some smoke, either marijuana or hash. Usually a person is left alone.

Steve began coming to the Shenendoah as part of his research for the investigative article, but it has also become a habit with him, a quiet hideaway when the outside world becomes too much too bear. He has spent more and more of his time cloistered in this darkness, spending the proceeds of his nocturnal adventure in a dusky world of smoke and coloured light. As he has encountered successive blind alleys both in his research for articles and in his search for the truth about his encounter with the two policemen, he has spent less and less time with his nose in the newspaper and more time with it tucked in an upturned glass of beer.

Today is no exception. After planning to rise at seven to begin work, he did not actually get out of bed until ten thirty. By the time he had walked to Kresge's and read the Globe and Mail over breakfast the morning was almost gone. He had walked home and spent a couple of hours reshuffling his newspaper clippings and thinking about washing the stacked dirty dishes from the previous two days. In the end he had really accomplished nothing, and by one thirty he was ready for a quick beer. He had started out to walk to Geno's outdoor patio, a short jaunt from his apartment, but thought that he may as well duck into the Shenendoah, not much further away and offering entertainment for just ten cents more on the price of a bottle of beer. At three o'clock, Marj has just brought Steve his fourth bottle of Old Vienna and he is quite relaxed as he watches Coco, bathed in soft blue light, caress the stage to a disco rhythm.

"Mind if I sit down?"

"Go 'head."

"Lansing?"

"What?" Steve sits up, feet on the floor, and turns to peer through the hazy air at his new table mate, "Oh, it's you. Sta..."

"Peter. Please, just Peter. I'm not sure I should even be talking to you, so I'd rather not have any other names come out. Just Peter, and let's keep our voices down, okay?"

"What is this?"

"Listen, Lansing. I just want to help you, that's all."

"Help. How can you help me?"

"Something's going on. I don't know quite what, but I have some ideas. I wanted to talk to you before, but there never seemed to be a chance with you always in public. Then the surveillance was taken off and you started coming in here pretty regular. I figured if I came in on my day off I could probably find you."

"You said surveillance. Then they were having me followed after all.?"

"Not officially, but yes."

"And?"

"Something's going on."

"You said that. What is going on? Why are you here?"

"Let me get a beer first, then we'll talk."

Staff Sergeant Goodman beckons to Marj, and when she comes to the table he orders a Canadian. When the beer has arrived and been paid for, he takes a couple of swallows directly from the bottle then begins again to talk to Steve.

"Anyway, like I said, something is going on. And I'm not sure I like it, even though I haven't yet quite figured it out. But it has to do with you, with that little problem you had, and a lot more besides."

"And? What else? What do you want from me?"

"Well, I thought I could help you. At least, let you know what's going on as far as I understand it. And maybe..."

"And maybe what? Why did you stop? What do you mean, and maybe?"

"Well, you're a civilian. You're outside the force. You might see or hear things that I wouldn't, things that pertain to what's happening inside the department. Maybe we could help each other. You know, sort of exchange information."

"I see."

Steve falls silent, letting his eyes slowly slip around the room, sliding across the rich hardwood mouldings bathed in satiny red light, almost as though he is caressing the fallen luxury of the room with his eyes. Peter Goodman waits.

"No. Maybe I don't see. What's in it for you? You're just a middle rank cop. You've got no authority to do anything about anything. So what's in it for you? You're not sneaking around like this for curiosity, so—what?"

"Guilt, I guess. Or something like it. I think you've been used, conned somehow. And I've been made a part of it. I'd like to try to clear it up, that's all."

"What can you do? Nothing! Unless...unless you're here to set me up. You guys were bugging me a long time, following and so on. Maybe it's not over! Maybe the method is just changed. Yeah, that's it. No, I don't think we have anything to talk about. Tell Farley that!"

"Listen, Lansing, I'm telling you the department didn't send me. Damn it, I just want to help. I can give you some information you might not find out any other way. And you're right about my rank, but if I can find evidence of any kind of wrongdoing in the department, there are people in Toronto I can go to. They'll send someone down from the government to take charge and investigate. But I don't have enough. I need your help from outside, okay?"

"I don't know..."

"Lansing, try it for a while. If anything bothers you about the arrangement, you can bail out at any time, eh?"

"Let me think about it."

"Okay, it's Tuesday today, how about if I check back with you Thursday around the same time?"

"Fine."

Steve is lost again in the smoke obscured hardwood finery of the Shenendoah, his face fixed in some lapsed thought as his eyes roll slowly around the room."

"What'd the cop want?"

It is Marj, her voice cutting through the haze, bringing Steve back to the table. He turns and sees that Peter Goodman is gone. He must have gotten up quietly and slipped out of the room into the afternoon sunshine, but to Steve it is almost as though he has dissolved into one of the wisps of smoke that fill the air around him.

"Huh?"

"Just curious, Steve. You can always tell a cop. I was just wondering if he was hassling you."

"No, just a guy I know."

"Oh."

"Listen, Marj, just forget you saw us together, okay? Same if you see him with me again. A favour for me?"

"Sure Steve."

Chapter Nineteen

In the false Eden of Timothy's, a bright windowed sunny downtown restaurant filled with big potted plants on the floor, plants hanging everywhere, festive floral wallpaper, and gay nineties decor, Steve and Janice are having lunch.

In the weeks since Steve's first telephone call and their subsequent meeting, their relationship has become much more than simply a common bond formed by the mystery of Rick Bergeron's disappearance and his connection to Steve's adventure. They have met often for lunch or supper and sometimes to take in a movie, and while they have discussed that common bond from time to time, more often they have not discussed it at all. Today is one of the exceptions.

As he and Janice sit in the sunlight filtering through the greenery of Timothy's, Steve brings up his unexpected meeting with Sergeant Goodman yesterday afternoon, repeating for her benefit, as best he can remember after finishing the evening drinking at the Shenendoah, the essence of the conversation. He stops at this point. They have both finished their meals and are on their second glass of wine. After a lengthy silence, Janice prods him.

"So, what are you going to do about it?"

"I don't know. Do you think it's a trick of some kind?"

"Could be. Who knows? But you know, you do get a bit paranoid about this stuff sometimes. Maybe it's worth taking a chance. I've never met this Goodman. What's he like?"

"Nice enough. He seems genuinely concerned, always did. Still, I don't know. Nothing's quite what it seems anymore."

"Well, if he seems okay, why not give him a chance. Just be wary. If he really wants to help, he can probably tell you a lot about the police you would never find out otherwise. If not, we can drop him. It's just a matter of being careful, right?"

"I guess so."

"So?"

"I'll meet him tomorrow and see what he says."

"Good."

Steve drives Janice back to Ford's then goes back to his apartment to look over his files one more time. He is home most of the afternoon, then he spends the evening at Janice Bergeron's, watching television and sharing with her two bottles of white wine. Thursday morning he drives Janice to work and then returns to his apartment to continue his attempt to make sense of his collected clippings and notes.

At two o'clock, in his usual frustration at a puzzle whose pieces never fit, he gives up. He walks to the Shenendoah Tavern and a cold beer.

Chapter Twenty

Shelley has just completed her set, going from sophisticated lady to buff tinged with blue light, reverse evolution in the time it takes the jukebox on stage to play four songs. Sara has just begun to shed her flowing sheers in the soft glow of rosy lights as Steve begins his second Old Vienna of the day. The clock above the pinball machine reads three ten.

"Hi."

"Hi, ah Peter."

"What did you decide?"

"Sit down."

"Thanks. I know this will work out. You won't be sorry."

"I hope not."

Steve pauses to examine Peter Goodman's features in the dimly lit haze. He sees a barely handsome man in his late thirties, considerably balding, with bright eyes and a sincere mouth. From their previous meetings, Steve knows that the Staff Sergeant is moderately heavy set, perhaps five nine and just under two hundred pounds by the look of him.

In fact, Peter Goodman is thirty seven years old, a twenty year veteran of first the Toronto and then the Windsor police forces who has risen to the rank of Staff Sergeant through honesty and diligence to his duty, often seeing other, less careful policemen speed past him when promotions were announced. Most of these he had seen fall as rapidly as they had risen, but a few had stayed on top. It was a situation Peter Goodman did not like—at all. Now he had been drawn into what seemed to be, at best, an irregular, certainly non-regulation if not exactly illegal situation. He is certain there is something going on that the police department should not be abetting. Try as he might, he has never been able to break the stereotype, the Toronto-Irish Catholic cop, the honesty inbred by the society he was raised in; coverups are not, have never been, his way. In this case, he has been made a part of it in some small way he still does not understand, but something inside him nags, will not allow him to just go along. Yet he lacks both the rank and the knowledge to do much at this point. It's like shooting at clouds in a night sky, yet he knows he must do what he can to set things right, even if some of the resulting flak falls back on his own head.

"Okay, now listen. I'll tell you what I know. Then if you have any questions or anything to add, fine."

"Go on."

"Okay. Right after you filed your complaint with me against the two policemen, who were unknown to us at that time, Chief Farley called me up to his office. He gave me the names of Butler and Porter and said they were the ones who had attacked you. He told me he had asked them to report to me the next day at two, and had himself placed them under suspension until after hearings could determine the degree of fault. He said he was sure they were guilty, to investigate but not to push the matter too far. He said it was very important to have the whole matter over and done with but to keep it low profile. It sounded kind of funny to me, but after all he is the chief! Anyway, I questioned them and I got the flashlight, from Butler's hands not his locker. Well, you know how the hearings went. They more or less made themselves look real guilty. What could Urizen do but find them at fault? But here's what's funny: I don't really recall seeing either of them before our first meeting and I haven't seen them since the hearings. So I checked. A friend of mine works with the computers. He ran them down in the files—or rather he didn't. Apparently there are no such constables. Frank Porter and Les Butler do not exist, at least as far as the Windsor Police are concerned. And another thing, I don't buy that flashlight story. I have tried tossing one like that at home. His range was too far and too fast for him to have tossed that thing hard enough to have bust your window. I think he shot at you."

"Wait a minute! I saw those guys that night, and again at the hearings. Exactly what do you mean, they don't exist?"

"Just that they are not part of our department. I don't know what they have over the chief, but it looks like he asked me and a few others to help him with a coverup!"

"What else?"

"Not much. It's just that feeling I get that something is wrong with the whole thing. And it seems to be starting at the top."

"So that's why you want to talk to me? To help you investigate?"

"Yes."

"On your own? Aren't you asking for problems? Isn't there some sort of procedure for that? Internal investi- gators or provincial guys or something like that?"

"The thing is, I don't know how high this goes. I know I can't talk to the chief. Who told him what to do? Who is it safe for me to go to? I don't know. If we can get enough information to start a case, then I can find someone in Toronto to investigate—but first I need more than just hunches."

"Okay, I'll try to help. Like you said, we'll trade information. For now, do you know anything about Rick Bergeron?"

"Only that he works for Windsor Taxi and he took off a couple of months ago. His wife has called the station a few times. That's all."

"How about a guy called Wino? He might know Bergeron. That's all I know about him."

"Could be a guy, Bill Peterson, worked for the cab company too but quit about a month ago. Got a minor record, for pot, things like that, but the department thinks he's been into bigger things the last couple years. He drove and did some dispatch work for a small owner named Atracura. Peterson was called Wino a lot."

"Was?"

"Apparently he left town. Nobody has seen him since he quit his job. Heard he might be in T.O. or somewhere."

"What about the Buick? Why is it still following me?"

"What Buick?"

"Dark blue. Regal, I think. It's been following me ever since the night of the shooting. It's getting so I almost ignore it, like my shadow."

"You're sure?"

"Sure. Last night it followed me to Janice Bergeron's place. This morning it followed me back home. It's probably parked somewhere across the street right now."

"I don't know."

"Come on, Peter! I checked the plates against what I understand are the Mountic and provincial police license numbers. They don't match up. It must be a city car!"

"No, I'm sure of that. All ours are Fords, except for a couple of Chevies: no Buicks. Can you give me the plate numbers?"

"Yes. I'll write it down for you."

"Okay. I'll check it out and get back to you."

"Soon?"

"When I know. Meantime, don't try to contact me. Too risky."

Steve is sitting alone again in the red and yellow light that filters through the smoke around him. He turns his attention to the ebony form on the stage before him.

Chapter Twenty One

```
CONFIDENTIAL REPORT
TEUFEL: EYES ONLY
SUBJECT: LANSING, STEPHEN PERCIVAL
BORN: CALGARY, ALBERTA, CANADA, JANUARY 10,
1949
CANADIAN CITIZEN FROM BIRTH
FATHER: GEORGE MARKHAM LANSING, PIPEFITTER,
DECEASED 1960
MOTHER: MARILYN ANN LANSING, NEE ARNER,
WOMEN'S PAGE COLUMNIST, REGINA NEWS
MOST RECENT STATISTICS:
HEIGHT: 5 FEET 9-1/2 INCHES
WEIGHT: 170 POUNDS
HAIR: DARK BLOND TO LIGHT BROWN
EYES: BLUE
COMPLEXION: LIGHT
MARITAL STATUS: SINGLE
EDUCATION: UNIVERSITY OF ALBERTA,
EDMONTON
B.A. ENGLISH, 5 SEMESTERS,
INCOMPLETE
HENRY WISE WOOD HIGH SCHOOL,
CALGARY
GRADE 12, MATRICULATION,
B AVERAGE ON PROVINCIAL
DEPARTMENTAL EXAMINATIONS
```

FAIRVIEW JUNIOR HIGH SCHOOL,
CALGARY
GRADE 9, A- AVERAGE ON
PROVINCIAL DEPARTMENTAL
EXAMINATIONS
NORTH HILL ELEMENTARY SCHOOL,
CALGARY
GRADE 6, B AVERAGE
EMPLOYMENT: REPORTER, THE EDMONTON
JOURNAL, 1 YEAR
REPORTER, THE REGINA POST,
3 YEARS
MISCELLANEOUS, ABOUT THREE
YEARS INCLUDING PERIODS OF
UNEMPLOYMENT
ARRESTS: NONE
CONVICTIONS: NONE
TRAFFIC OFFENSES: SPEEDING, 1965 20 MPH O/L
1968 (2) 12 MPH O/L
15 MPH O/L
1973 14 MPH O/L
1975 15 MPH O/L
KNOWN CRIMINAL ASSOCIATIONS: NONE
PRIOR   INVESTIGATION: RCMP,   ROUTINE,
RECEIVING
"SOVIET UNION TODAY"
AND OTHER LEFTIST
PUBLICATIONS,
CORRESPONDING WITH
SUSPECTED RADICAL
ORGANIZATIONS, PART
TIME COLUMNIST FOR
"RYCE STREET FISH
MARKET"
UNDERGROUND
NEWSPAPER,
SURVEILLANCE COMPLETED AUGUST 1968,
RESULTS INCONCLUSIVE

```
LAST KNOWN EMPLOYMENT: UNEMPLOYED
LAST KNOWN RESIDENCE: 321 RIVERSIDE DRIVE
E
UPR
WINDSOR, ONTARIO
N9A 6T6
TELEPHONE: (519) 295-6661
VEHICLE: FORD CUSTOMLINE HT, 1956,
WHITE ON RED
PLATE CRZ 252 ONTARIO
NO FURTHER INFORMATION AVAILABLE
ON SUBJECT AT THIS TIME
WILL FORWARD INFORMATION AS IT COMES
AVAILABLE
COPY CMDR PAZITCH HQ OTTAWA
END OF INFORMATION
XNTF 3851 B2
```

***

The man in the driver's seat of the blue car looks at his partner, who has just looked up from reading three attached computer sheets received in the morning's mail.

"What do you make of that?"

"I guess he's not too likely to become a problem after all, eh Frank?"

"I don't know. There's nothing really criminal in his background, but he does have those radical connections. And it is suspicious the way he just happened to be in our way like that. I don't know."

"Yeah, but the Mounties investigated those radical tie-ins and never found anything. Besides, that's close to ten years ago and nothing since. And outside of speeding, he doesn't seem to have had much to do with the law. Looks to me like he's clean."

"He still seems to be trying too hard. The whole thing should be over as far as he's concerned, but he keeps poking around, asking questions. Maybe he's just been clever, covered his tracks well. We really haven't got much information on him yet. Until we can fill him out, find out for sure who he is, I think we'll continue to keep an eye on him."

"What about the yankee?"

"Until we get another communication, we don't know where he is or what he's doing. We have to stick around and wait anyway, so while we are in Windsor we'll watch Lansing. Besides, from the looks of it, he's trying to track down the yankee himself, through that Bergeron woman and through Atracura's cabs. Who knows, he may lead us to our target himself."

"I suppose so."

"We'll wait until we get another lead on the yankee anyway, then we'll see about Lansing."

Frank Toefel slips the folded computer sheet back into its white envelope and lays it on the seat between him and his partner. For the rest of the morning they remain parked in the railway freight yard across from 321 Riverside Drive East, watching and waiting.

Chapter Twenty Two

Wednesday: nearly a week since Steve last spoke with Peter Goodman. Janice Bergeron is awakened by an insistant ringing of her doorbell. When she has found her robe and groped her way downstairs to answer the door, she finds herself facing a darkly dressed man, probably middle aged, who stands in the shadows to the side of the porch. As she reaches to turn on the porch light, he reaches out as though to stop her.

"Don't turn that on, please."

"Who are you?"

"Are you Mrs. Bergeron?"

"Yes."

"I am a friend of Steve Lansing. Will you be seeing him today, this morning?"

"Maybe. Why?"

"I want you to give him a message. Can you take this envelope with you to work? It's important that he gets the message this morning!"

"I can call..."

"Please. Don't mention the message on your telephone or his.   You could be overheard."

"I'll call and arrange to meet him for lunch. Okay?"

"Fine."

"Can I tell him who you are?"

"I would prefer not to say. Even here we might be seen, overheard. He'll know. He expects to hear from me."

"Then I think I know too. I'll keep Quiet."
"Thank you."

***

It is exactly twelve noon according to the grandfather clock in the corner at Timothy's as Steve moves past the line of people waiting to be seated and walks to the table Janice has already claimed for them. She has a look that tells him this lunch has as much to do with business as with pleasure.
"Hi. What's up?"
"He came. This morning, to my place with a message."
"Who came. Slow down please."
"Your friend Peter. He doesn't want us to be too free with his name in public. He seemed scared."
"So what did he say?"
"Nothing."
"Nothing at all?"
"No. But he left this. Said you must have it today."
She hands Steve a note size envelope with nothing written on it, not even his name. He turns it over very slowly, then rips it open and unfolds the small piece of paper he finds inside. He reads it over slowly then passes it to Janice so that she may read it too.

> *I have your information. Must see you but not the same place. Call 259-8815 between noon and two. Do not say your name or mine. I'll tell you where we meet. This is very important!*

"I'd better call. I'll be back in a minute."
Taking the note from Janice, he walks out of Timothy's and crosses the street to the Cardinal Inn, where there are pay telephones in the basement but usually no people to overhear a

67

private conversation. Steve has noted these telephones before, just in case he picked up confidential leads for his investigative article. Now his foresight is paying off in an unexpected way. He drops in twenty cents and dials. The telephone rings eight times and he is about to give up when the receiver is finally picked up at the other end.

"Hello."

"It's me."

"Are you somewhere private?"

"Basement of the Cardinal, at a pay phone. No one can get anywhere near without me seeing them. What's all this hush hush stuff? Isn't the Shenendoah private enough?"

"Not now."

"Why not? What's happening?"

"I'd rather tell you in person. Nothing on the phone. Nothing in writing."

"Where do we meet? And when?

"Can you lose the Buick?"

"I'll work something out."

"We have to get out of town. Do you know where County Road 19 crosses Highway 3?"

"Yeah. That's pretty far out of town, isn't it?"

"It's far enough they won't find us easily. And the country is flat. We can see anybody coming for miles around!"

"if you feel it's necessary, okay. How does five thirty or so sound?"

"Late."

"I can make it earlier if you like. It's just that Janice is off at four thirty, so it will be easier to lose my tail."

"Okay, five thirty."

"Listen, is all this cloak and dagger stuff really necessary?"

"It's urgent. Believe it!"

Steve returns to Janice and discusses his telephone call inwhispers over a fresh vegetarian lunch. He has already developed a plan to help him keep his appointment without being followed. He explains to Janice the role she can play in his scheme. After lunch Janice drives her Vega back to Ford's and Steve walks back to his apartment to resume work on his colossal and ever more complicated puzzle.

Chapter Twenty Three

At four thirty, Steve takes a surreptitious peek from the corner of his bay window: the Buick is still parked across the street. He walks downstairs and outside, gets into his car and turns left onto Riverside Drive. At Ouellette Avenue, as he begins another left hand turn, he can see that the Buick is following and has already started to signal left. He turns left again at Pitt Street and selects a parking spot about halfway down the one way street. He gets out of the car and, with a quick sideways glance as he enters Mossman's Delicatessen, confirms that the Buick is slipping into a parking spot on the opposite side of the street to his own. He walks briskly the length of the long, narrow restaurant to the rear exit, walks outside and crosses the small city park behind the building to Chatham Street and the waiting Vega.

After a quick good luck kiss, Janice will walk back to Steve's apartment to wait for his return. Steve takes the Vega, turning left onto Ouellette Avenue, heading away from downtown Windsor andthe Detroit skyline, following Ouellette until it takes a broad curve and becomes Dougall then takes a longer and tighter curve to fork into Highway 401 and as quickly fork out again as Highway 3 toward Leamington. Halfway between this junction and the bedroom town of Essex, Steve turns right, drives up Essex County Road 19 for about a hundred yards and stops the car. Frequent checks of the rear view mirror have assured him that nobody has followed, and especially that the Buick must still be waiting for him to finish his supper at Mossman's. He shuts off the engine and gets out of the car.

Looking around, he sees that Peter Goodman was right; in opposite directions along Highway 3 he can see both the town of Essex and the skyline of Windsor; behind the car he can see Windsor again, several miles away along County Road 19, a major link between the east end of the city and Highway 3; in front of the car, along the unpaved, little used section of County Road 19, he sees only empty fields spotted here and there with windbreaks or distant farmhouses. He will be well forewarned of anyone approaching, will see them when they are still miles away in fact. He feels very alone in all this flatness, very vulnerable. Walking down the road a way, he cuts gingerly across the marshy bottom of the drainage ditch on the right side of the road and moves into the relative shelter of the wooded windbreak.

***

He is still there, leaning against a poplar, ten minutes later when a second car turns the corner, drives slowly past the Vega, then pulls to the side of the road. The driver hesitates a few seconds, then steps cautiously out of the car, leaving the door open and the motor running. Steve recognizes the sturdy form of Peter Goodman and steps out of the poplar grove. He recrosses the ditch and walks down the road toward the policeman, who stays beside his car, hand on the door as though about to bolt. Only when Steve has almost reached him does the other man attempt what might seem a smile if it did not look so grim.

"Hi, Peter. What's this all about? Why all the secrecy?"

"Trouble, that's what!"

"Enough to sneak all over the county? Come on! Really, what did you find out?"

"It's the Buick. It's trouble, Steve, trouble! I don't know quite what you've started here Steve, but it's big, and I have a feeling it's bad! I think we're both in way over our heads!"

"What's that supposed to mean?"

"I mean it's probably too late to back out. Even if we wanted to!"

"Out of what? What about the Buick? What's happening, Peter?"

"Okay. I checked. You're right, the plates aren't Mountie or O.P.P., but they're definitely not ours either. I was able to check all that right in the department. So then I went back to my friend with the computer, and I went to the Department of Transport. I think it is a police car, but I don't know whose."

"What? It is a police car; it isn't a police car. One or the other! If it is, you should know who it belongs to, right?"

"Not this one."

"I don't understand."

"I don't either, quite. But I think I am starting to sort it out. This car is registered in Ottawa, to a federal agency. That's what makes it hard to track down; this is a do nothing agency, just a name. I did some further checking with some people I know in Ottawa. It seems this agency mostly serves as a licensing base for cars, firearms, and so on, when other agencies don't want to be identified with actions they are involved in."

"A cover."

"How's that?"

"A cover. You know, like spy stories."

"Yes, sort of, a place where federal and provincial policing agencies can get vehicles which are not readily traced to them. A safeguard against people like your friends who know all the license plate sequences."

"I'm not that important. Why are they following me?"

"I don't know. I think you may have stumbled into whatever they are working on somehow; maybe the shooting..."

"...and me being so stubborn about following up. After they tried so hard to cover up."

"I think so."

"Is that it?"

"No, I got a bit more, not much, from the computer. According to our records here, that car does not exist, no more than do the two guys who shot at you. There were no special cases being investigated. We drew a blank. So my friend did me a favour. We used another code to question a couple of computers in T.O. and Ottawa."

"And?"

"Only bits and pieces of inconsistent information. Piecing them together, my friend and I figure there is an investigation, a big one. We fed in the Buick and Wino and Bergeron. We got back more names. Teufel and Malenfant, apparently police, but no indication of rank or of who they work for, and Atracura. We fed it in again including these names, and we got back a bit more. The name Frank Lazlo, and an American computer entry key. We could have used that too, but we don't know where the computer is located."

"So? What does all that mean?"

"I'm not sure. But if it's important enough that they have to hide the identities of their investigators even from the local police, then it is pretty big. And if Frank Lazlo's in it...!"

"Who is Lazlo?"

"Yankee. Lives in Detroit. No one knows everything he's into. They say he mostly sells power. Rumour has it he runs some prostitution rings, gay and straight both, and he has a lot to do with drug traffic across the border. Some people say he's into big time counterfeiting, and murder for hire. In fact, there's not much people don't say he's into. But none of it has ever been proved. He's been investigated, arrested, always got off. They have gotten a few of his associates, but even that is rare. Still, if he is involved in something, it's gotta be big—into the millions!"

"Sounds like!"

"Listen. A few years ago, it was even rumoured that he planned to take over a Caribbean island, make it a sort of private kingdom, a haven for gambling and other underworld activities. It never happened, but still...."

"Mafia?"

"No one even knows what that is, but he has no obvious connection with any of those guys, seems to be totally independent. And more powerful that any of them. None of them are untouchable, but he seems to be. No, if he has any special connections, they are elsewhere."

"So what do we do now?"

"Like I said, it's big. And that probably means dangerous! You can try and get out if you'd like. Maybe it's not too late to drop it."

"And you?"

"It still bothers me the way they are going about things, the way they handled your case for instance. There's something funny going on. I don't like it."

"You're not going to quit?"

"No. I can't."

"You still want help outside?"

"It's dangerous. Too many people are disappearing: Rick Bergeron, Wino Peterson."

"I still want to know about the other car, about why I was shot at."

"It's dangerous."

"I know. What do we do now."

"Keep on as you were. I'll work out a way we can keep in touch and get back to you."

The grey shadows of dusk are beginning to surround the two men as they get back into their cars, the poplars painting grotesque black forms across the narrow dirt road. Each backs to the highway, then the policeman crosses the highway, disappearing rapidly down County Road 19 toward the city. Steve points the Vega westward, back the way he has come, along Highway 3. Ahead of him he can see the skyline, more Detroit than Windsor, silhouetted against the growing fiery dome of summer sunset.

Chapter Twenty Four

Janice is standing by the bay window looking out at the deepening crimson of the Detroit River as the Vega turns into the driveway next to the building. She walks back to the kitchen and pours two cups of coffee while Steve parks and comes up the stairs.

"Hi, I thought you'd like some coffee."

"Good. Thanks."

"So what happened?"

"I met him. The Buick didn't follow."

"Didn't come here either. What did he say?"

"Not much, really. He's been doing some checking. It looks like I've got into something pretty big, pretty strange too."

"What does that mean? Strange?"

"Well, it looks like those guys in the Buick are some kind of secret government cops, undercover guys like in the movies. And they're looking into something that involves your husband, and Wino, and their boss, plus some gangster in Detroit. Even the city cops don't know about them."

"So how does Goodman know?"

"I guess he took a chance on some unorthodox channels, computers and so on."

"So now what?"

"I don't know. Goodman's going to get back to me, eh."

"Then?"

"I guess we'll keep digging, but...listen, he thinks this is big enough and important enough that it could get dangerous. Maybe you should just stay out."

"Steve, I'm in. Whether I like it or not. Rick took care of that, and you."

"I suppose so. I'm sorry for that."

"Don't be."

"I don't think Rick's coming back."

"I know."

Steve and Janice finish their coffee and walk over to Geno's for a supper of pasta, then walk back in the settling darkness to her car and drive back to the townhouse in the east end of Windsor. They watch some television together. In the morning, Janice drives Steve back to his Ford, still parked in front of Mossman's Delicatessen, and goes on to work.

***

For several weeks now, Janice has been sleeping well. Thursday night is different. Steve is working on his clippings at home. She is alone in the townhouse and worn out from an exceptionally busy day at work. By ten o'clock she is ready to seek the comfort of sleep, but she holds out until eleven, then falls asleep with the novel she is reading still in her hand. Tonight she sleeps fitfully. She has been drawn deeper into that other world that sometimes envelopes her at night, so that she becomes like a Gypsy lady trapped inside her own glowing glass globe. The alarm seems more to shriek than to ring her awake on a warm, sunlit Friday morning. She is shivering.

Janice quickly leaves her bed, finds her robe, and telephones Steve; she must talk to someone. She feels very alone. She must talk to Steve.

Chapter Twenty Five

Although it is long after midnight, the cities have not achieved total blackness, being domed on this summer night, as is always the case, by a pale blue corona of light from the streets. Blackness comes in the form of a Cadillac Seville, rising from the American city through the gracious arc of the Ambassador Bridge then descending as quickly through the shadows to Canada. Just over fifteen minutes later it hushes, lights off, up to a garage door in prestigious South Windsor. As the door rises, the Cadillac slips into the complementary darkness beyond, and the door closes behind. Three dark forms pass through the connecting doorway and up the stairs, through the spacious unlit kitchen into the well appointed living room of Lucio Atracura's home.

"Sit down please, gentlemen. Will you have some coffee? A drink?"

"This isn't a social call, Bud."

"I know. I just thought..."

"Okay, okay. A scotch might go good. Rocks."

"Okay. You Rudy?"

"You gotta beer?"

"Sure."

The good host walks back into the kitchen, returning momentarily with a bottle of Carlsberg and a glass, which he sets on the table in front of the man called Rudy. Then he goes to the credenza, pouring a Jack Daniels on the rocks for Frank Lazlo and a Courvoisier for himself, straight up, and returns to take a seat opposite his two guests.

77

"Okay, Bud, now we have to talk."

"What's the problem, Frank?"

"You know the problem as well as I do."

"That Lansing guy."

"He been asking you any more questions?"

"No. He called that one time about Bergeron. I gave him Bergeron's home number and he hasn't called back. I think he's seeing Bergeron's old lady now though."

"And her. Has she called?"

"Not recently. She called a few times right after he disappeared, then she stopped. She called the cops too, but when they came I just told them he stopped showing up for work. No problem."

"Wrong. It is a problem."

"What do you mean?"

"What I mean is, I had Rudy do some checking for me. Had him look into this Lansing a bit. Rudy, tell Bud about Lansing."

"Well, it seems that even before Lansing had his run in with the cops he was hanging around a few places in town, asking questions. I guess he was trying to be subtle about it, but he's not that slick, and people figured he was after an organization, one like ours by the sound of his questions. He fancies he's a writer, so he could be trying to do a story. On the other hand, he never seems to do any writing, so maybe he's a cop. I don't know. The thing is his questions started before the shooting, before Bergeron left us. And another thing, I had a couple of guys watch him for a while. Funny. It seems somebody else is watching him too, two guys. They watch his place when he's home, follow him when he leaves. We haven't been able to find out who they are yet or who they're working for. On top of that, Lansing has been having secret meetings with a cop. Why? Is he working with them?"

"If he was, why would they shoot at him?"

"Who knows? Maybe to throw us off. Anyway, he's still asking around town about us, or someone very like us. And there's that cop."

"So what do we do, Frank?"

"I'm not sure there is much we can do right now. If he disappears, we may raise a whole hornet's nest of questions. Rudy has made sure nobody who knows about us will tell him anything. Just so we're aware that he hasn't quit. And we have to find out who else is interested, who those other two guys are. That's all."

"Just sit on it?"

"That's right. And hope we can solve the problem."

The three men sit in silence for a few minutes, then Frank Lazlo moves the conversation to the next item on the agenda.

"Bud, my people in Montreal have been in touch again."

"Another shipment?"

"Yes, soon."

"Is it wise, with all this heat?"

"It has to be done. If anyone gets in the way, we'll have to take care of it, that's all."

"Same way as last time?"

"Maybe, I'll let you know. Just be ready to move quickly. I may call you on very short notice. You got any drivers you can trust?"

"I'll have someone ready. No problem."

"You said Bergeron was no problem."

"I was mistaken."

"No more mistakes. Period."

"I'll have someone I can trust."

"After this, Rudy will contact you."

Something conclusive in the softening of Frank Lazlo's voice signals Bud Atracura that the meeting has ended. It seems to him that nothing has really been resolved. He wonders why his American contact had felt such a meeting important enough to hold at this late hour. Something compels him to ask again.

"When will I hear?"

"About?"

"The delivery."

"Don't worry about it. Just you and your people play it cool. There are too many questions. You'll hear from Rudy when we're ready."

"And the Lansing thing?"

"Like I said, we'll keep an eye on him. Nothing more."

"I don't like it."

"Neither do I, but that's all we can do for now: wait."

Together the three walk back through the kitchen and down the stairs into the murk of the attached garage. Bud Atracura presses the switch to open the garage door as his erstwhile guests settle into the blackness of the Cadillac. Within seconds, he is left alone in the dark garage.

Chapter Twenty Six

It is what many people would call an ideal Friday morning. The sky is bright blue and clear, with only a smattering of misty clouds. The sun is high and seems to smile benevolently on all below, unobscured by the haze of pollutants which so often seems to fill the Windsor air. All the city seems to have suddenly come to life in the comfort of seventy degrees blown clear of the usually cloying humidity by a light breeze off the Detroit River. A young mime artist, temporarily out of work, practices his craft in whiteface and painter's coveralls over black dancer's tights, hoping to be noticed and hired by some creative businessman. From the riverfront to Wyandotte Street and back again he beguiles adults and children alike with feats of magical sleight of hand and enthrals them with his facial and bodily contortions. Halfway along the mime's route sits the birdman, a fiftyish gentleman in raggedy clothes with a long artificial flower bobbing from his battered fedora in unconscious mimicry of Emmett Kelly. In his hands he has a child's toy, one of those plastic pipes shaped like a thrush which, when filled partially with water and blown through, warbles with a loud birdlike sound. Beside him is a bowl with enough water to easily last the whole day as he delights passers by as he fills the street with his pseudo woodland sounds. The young ladies expose enough fleshly delights among them to thrill each of the young men as they in turn parade the street with flexings of biceps and flashings of teeth and flauntings of hair, every one showing his or her best to advantage. The street is a happy summer festival leading to and from Dieppe Gardens, the park itself a reprise of that scene, slowed down slightly as strollers stop to watch the river traffic flowing by or gaze at the Detroit skyline, highlighted by the futuristic towers of the chrome plated Renaissance Center on the east and the century old Bob-Lo boats, really full sized triple decker riverboats, on the west end, tapering off beyond these landmarks into the distance, and the bridges: Belle Isle in the east connected to Detroit but not to Canada, and Ambassador in the West tying the two nations for better or for worse. Today the traffic throngs that bridge in both directions not only with the lifeblood of commerce but with thousands of happy families seeking summer pastimes in a foreign land, revelling in nature's generosity.

***

Bud Atracura has slept late. It is nearly ten o'clock and the light of the summer sun that filters through cracks around the drawn blinds of his South Windsor bedroom has not yet penetrated his dark sleep. His wife and children are visiting her sister in Toronto, so there is no one in the house to wake him, and he was up very late last night so Bud has allowed himself the rare pleasure of sleeping late. As the clock radio reaches ten the alarm goes off in unfriendly tones then, just as an arm reaches toward it, shuts off, giving way to the mellow sounds of CJOM, the Windsor FM station. The arm is withdrawn and Bud Atracura opens his eyes and halfway sits up, leaning on one arm. As soon as he has become accustomed to being awake, he gets out of bed and dresses, then he opens the designer blinds his wife has selected for the bedroom, wincing at the sudden incursion of sunlight as the first one snaps upward.

It is a bright, sunny day, a good day for relaxing, and the cars will take care of themselves. Bud has given the drivers their assignments for today already. But Bud is not receptive to the festive atmosphere filling the Windsor air. He has other matters to attend to. Spurning his home telephone, he goes to a pay telephone in a nearby shopping centre. After making several calls, he returns home and relaxes for about an hour. At noon, he drives downtown and dines at the Auberge de la Bastille, a popular steak house. He has reserved a table in a room that is set off from the rest, a private table where several men and women, all stylishly dressed, join him for lunch. The meeting touches on the need for security, for extra care, without revealing any more than necessary of the previous evening's conclave.

After lunch there is time to enjoy the start of another weekend. The others will let their minions know of the new necessity for strictures on information; the drivers will not report in until tonight, and Bud can talk to them then. In the meantime, he will relax with a beer or two and enjoy summer while he can.

***

As Bud Atracura settles into the comfort of a redwood chaise lounge in the cool shade of his backyard patio, word has already been telephoned from Detroit to Montreal: the difficulties have been resolved, the situation taken care of; all is well in Windsor. With the assurances of their contact, Rudy Noiraud, that all is well, the people in Montreal are ready to resume the transactions begun so many weeks before with the transfer of that one portentous box from Detroit into the hands of Rick Bergeron. Rudy has taken the liberty, or perhaps one should say the precaution, of guaranteeing security not in his own name or that of Frank Lazlo but in the name of Lucio Atracura.

Chapter Twenty Seven

It is a pleasant spring day, with the sunshine flowing from the bright blue sky like liquid gold and the wisps of cloud repeating the white beauty of the delicate flowers that seem to abound in the green of the meadow. A lone hawk wheels gracefully above groves of trees that cast their shade at irregular intervals in all directions like havens for travellers who may pass this way. Janice and Steve are walking hand in hand through the meadow, enjoying the pristine beauty that surrounds them. The air is filled with birdsong and floral scent and their minds are filled with nothing so much as a blissful, eternal calm. There is no need to speak because their minds are one with each other and with this Eden they walk.

As they walk, a gentle breeze wafts through the mid-calf deep grass, running rilling waves as far as the eye can see. All is well with the world and the world is at peace.

At the far edge of the world, at the very rim of the rippling waves of grass and white flowers, in the most distant of the shading shibboleths of trees, one of the shadows moves with the breeze blown swaying of the boughs, seems almost to move of its own will, to grow and to rise wraithlike from the horizon.

In the silence of this spring day, Steve raises his hand palm-upward as he glances at Janice, and a droplet of water appears as mysteriously as the dew. They both know the rain will start soon, so they start toward the nearest of the wooded groves, seeking shelter. It begins as a light shower, cool and refreshing to the strolling couple as they head for the protection of spreading deciduous branches. There is a primeval wonder at the changeability of the heavens filling their minds as the infrequent drops slip to earth.

In the distance, at the horizon and even beyond, there grows a seeming meadow of grey misty wraiths rising into the darkening sky as the rain intensifies. With still a distance to walk before they will reach the trees ahead, Janice and Steve each notice the suddenness of the shift in environment. What had been a caressing breeze now blows and billows, swirls and whirls like some destructive mountebank dancing shaman to the rain. And the rain that was a trickle now has grown to deluge proportions, soaking, smothering everything everywhere and, abetted by the remnant heat of the sun, turning everywhere to obscuring mists rising from the earth. In the distance, through the haze, Janice can see the dark shadows that have moved from under the shading trees have filled the sky as raincloud and are now an army of hominid forms marching from all directions toward Steve and her. As they hurry toward their sheltering grove, she can see that it too has become a mass of groping, menacing forms. There is nowhere to turn.

Turning, she sees that Steve is still surging forward, seeing nothing, a blind man in a momentum of remembered sight. She must act as guide. But where can she lead? There is nowhere to go, and on every hand the black forms move ever nearer. She must do something! Taking her Tiresias by the hand she turns toward what she assumes must be the east and begins to walk, hoping the wind will blow the rain toward the west, although she does not know why she thinks it will. They walk a watery vision of hell until the minion wraiths are near enough to reach and touch, grasp and grope, and grab!

At the very instant these living wisps are about to envelope Janice and her charge the rainbow appears, just ahead, slicing through the mists, parting the watery demons in a stroke to allow the two pilgrims to pass through. Janice leads on between the walls of shadows, toward the waiting rainbow. As they reach the radiant curved column of light, it seems to Janice a solid edifice etched with stairlike grips leading heavenward. Seeing nowhere else to lead her unsighted charge, she grasps one of the recessions, placing Steve's hand in another. They begin to climb toward the sky, still unseen beyond the massed black of the destructive nimbus.

Almost as though they had never been anywhere else, Janice and Steve are above the storm, above the clouds, standing on the edge of the rainbow, which has now become a bridge, each end rooted in the mists below. Steve points downward, his sight apparently restored, at the now desolated meadow they have left behind. She follows his direction and sees a man where they have once stood. He is afraid. The misty forms engulf him. He is drowning in their watery grasp. He disappears in a profusion of brightly coloured bubbles that gradually turn from rainbow hues to blue and then fade to nothingness.

She does not know what Steve is thinking. He has frozen in position, his right hand still pointing downward over the edge of the bridge. She senses more than sees that they are joined on this rainbow bridge by others, unidentifiable forms, white and misty against the gentle blue of the sky. In their presence she feels at ease.

Below, through occasional breaks in the black cover of cloud, she can see people, too distant to be recognized, each alone in a small and shrinking circle of meadow surrounded by menacing moving mists. She is horrified at the thought that she can see but she cannot help. She feels trapped in the glass globe of the sunlit sky, clear in her vision but unable to reach out to others drowning for want of that vision.

The white mists around her give her the assurance that she has at least been able to lend her sight to one person when his need was greatest, and that that is perhaps all she can ask. As she looks down again, the world below vanishes, destroyed in a clamour of clanging bells and shrieking sirens. Janice is awake, shivering in her sunlit bed.

Chapter Twenty Eight

POSSIBLE OVERDOSE WINDSOR CAB DRIVER DROWNED IN RIVER

Early yesterday morning the body of William David Peterson, a former driver and dispatch operator for the Windsor Taxi Company, was found in the Detroit River by two local children, apparently after having been in the water for several weeks.

John Reynolds, aged twelve, and his ten year old brother Tommy, had intended to go fishing at about six o'clock Wednesday morning when a snagged hook led them to their gruesome discovery. Following the line to trace their hook, the boys found the body of Mr. Peterson, more commonly known around Windsor as just "Wino," lodged against the pilings at the foot of the Canadian end of the Ambassador Bridge. A fire department rescue unit was called to retrieve the body.

A preliminary autopsy was completed late this morning and, according to police spokesmen, showed that there were high concentrations of the drug Librium present in the body but that the immediate cause of death was probably drowning, about three to four weeks ago.

Police do not discount the possibility that an overdose of Librium may have caused or contributed to Mr. Peterson's death, but they are satisfied that this is an unfortunate drowning accident, only possibly drug related. Foul play is not suspected.

***

It is early on a Friday morning and, fortified with a lukewarm cup of coffee, Steve has been poring over Thursday's Star, at least until the last several minutes. In the midst of an article on page three his gaze has rivetted, frozen on one word: "Wino."

The persistent ringing of the telephone finally breaks the bond between Steve's eyes and the black typography. He rises slowly, almost as though dazed, from the chesterfield in the living room and walks blindly toward the sound of the telephone in the kitchen. He picks up the receiver and places it to his ear but does not speak.

"Steve? Steve, is that you?"

"Huh? Oh, yeah. Hi Janice."

"Steve? Are you all right?"

"I'm okay, just thinking, that's all."

"Are you sure? You sound funny."

"I'm all right. How are you? Why are you calling?"

"I had a dream. I'm lonely. I just wanted to talk."

"Just a dream? One of your dreams? Which?"

"I had one of my dreams—I don't know what it means. I'm scared, Steve."

"Can you come over? Or I'll go over there? I have something I want to show you anyway."

"I'll come. I have to go to work anyway. I'll just call in and tell them I'll be a bit late. That'll give us an hour or so. I just need to be with you for a while, that's all."

"Good, I'll have the coffee on. And you can tell me all about this dream of yours."

"I'll be there in half an hour. Bye."

Steve returns to the living room, more awake now, and carefully clips the newspaper story about a taxi driver who is known as Wino, then he makes a fresh pot of coffee and waits for Janice to arrive. He knows dreams like hers have to be created from the stuff of the real world around the dreamer, yet these dreams give an uncanny illusion of being prophetic. He wishes it were easier for him to prove to Janice that what she has dreamed has entered her mind through normal associations of the media and the world she lives in, not through some sort of mysterious agency.

88

When Janice arrives, she looks drawn and tired, almost as though large portions of her blood had been drained away from her during the night, leaving only a much whiter shell of herself. Steve has her sit on the chesterfield, then he serves two coffees and sits beside her. Janice tells him what she remembers of the dream that has left her confused and worried. Dreams may be only subconscious reflections of a person's own conception of the real world, but Janice still believes that she saw her Uncle Barney on the morning he died, actually saw his ascension to heaven. How then can she be expected to believe any less in the dreams that describe to her events before they happen, that show her people before she meets them, that more than just seem to forecast, that actually do show Janice the future. Janice always knows a dream of prophesy when it happens.

Steve is ready with his arguments, designed to calm Janice's apprehensions, knowing full well that Janice will continue to believe that from time to time she can see the future in her dreams. He sits quietly, coffee in hand, as he listens to her recital of the most recent of her dreams. When she finishes, Steve has a look Janice does not quite understand, a look different than the usual fatherly style he affects when dealing with her dreams. She waits a few seconds, then grows impatient.

"Well?"

"I don't know. I just don't know, Janice."

"That's different."

"What?"

"No lecture on the nature of reality."

"Listen, Janice, did you watch TV at all last night?"

"A little. Why?"

"News?"

"No."

"You're sure?"

"Positive. What is it?"

"I just want to know. How about the paper? Did you read the paper last night?"

"No."

"How about the radio news?"

"No. I was reading. I had the CBC on—music all night."

"You're sure? No news?"
"Come on, Steve! What is this? I'm sure already."
"Remember when you called?"
"Mmmn."
"I said I had something to show you."
"Yes."
"Here, read this."

Steve pokes two fingers into his shirt pocket and fishes out the story he has just clipped from last night's paper. He hands it to Janice. As she reads, her already pale face pales more and her jawline hardens grimly as she begins to understand the questions about her reading, viewing, and listening habits. When she has finished, she sits, saying nothing for a moment and then only a word.

"Wino."
"Yes, Wino. Drowned."

Chapter Twenty Nine

On Saturday morning, when Steve and Janice wake to bright sunlight and the sound of Detroit River traffic, both are ready to flee from the world that impinges on all sides into the freedom of nature. It takes them only a few minutes over coffee to decide to drive into the countryside and only a few minutes more to make their excursion a trip to the island of Bob-Lo, a recreational park near Amherstburg, about a thirty minute drive away.

Having first outfitted themselves with a thermos of orange juice, moderately laced with vodka, a second thermos filled with coffee, and a picnic lunch of sandwiches and salad, they start out in Steve's old Ford, driving westward along Riverside Drive to where it blends with University Avenue to form old Sandwich Street which in turn becomes Highway 18 encircling Essex County.

They drive along Highway 18 between vast stands of trees, forested city parks, past the racetrack with its broad, flat parking lot wasteland, and around an intricate S-curve centred by a small bridge, into and through the village of LaSalle. Beyond LaSalle stretches miles of farms and forests, fruit stands and fish sellers, flea markets and marinas, lending this road a festive atmosphere in the brightness of the morning sunshine.

Just before River Canard the river begins to show through the trees on the right, its blue blending into the brightness of the sky above. Just beyond, the marshlands begin, with their profusion of wild birds and black American fishermen bringing life to a quiet land. Passing the two landmarks, a service station on the left and a tavern on the right, that define River Canard for the casual traveller, they come to the bridge that crosses the major portion of the marsh. They decide to stop for a few minutes and enjoy the air. From the top of the concrete structure, Steve and Janice can see the homes built out over the water on gravel and garbage outcroppings, protected by groynes and breakwaters, surrounded by small boats and barbeques. They can see the black families grouped along the shore below, fishing as though they had always been there, eternal as the shore itself, less foreign here than in their own land. They can see one of the Bob-Lo boats, the Columbia, churning its way through the hazel waters of the Detroit River.

Turning to face landward, they can see the flatness of Essex County, stretching seemingly forever, fanning outward from the bridge, the centre mostly water-spotted marshy clumps of high grasses and cattails, ducks sporadically flying upward or diving for food, sometimes trailed by beaked fluffballs of black and yellow across the water, the water growing less and the land more until fields of corn and other grains flow to the horizon and beyond, spotted here and there by cloud shaped clumps of forest dark against the blue.

Just as they are about to leave, although they have not noticed him before this, Janice sees a young man standing only a few yards ahead of the car, hitchhiking. She assumes that he must also be going to Bob-Lo because he is a mime, fully dressed in black tights and coveralls, with a small black derby, black brows and lips and black tear lines down the pure white of his face. She points him out to Steve and suggests that they offer him a ride. Steve agrees and the young magician travels with them the remainder of the way.

From the top of the bridge they descend into increasingly populated areas until finally they pass through the town of Amherstburg and park on a gravelled lot next to the highway. Walking with the mime through a tunnel under the highway, they take a small boat across a short stretch of murky water to the separate world that is Bob-Lo.

Once on the island, the young man with the white face moves into the crowds that cram the forty or so acres which are taken up with amusement activities, carnival booths, midway rides, craft shops, all the makings of any county fair. He appears and disappears in the flux of the living mass almost as miscellaneous objects appear and disappear under the skill of his nimble hands as he flows through the crowded park plying his special craft.

Steve and Janice opt for the open air, moving quickly through the crowds with only an occasional glance to either side as they head for the more than two hundred acres of open countryside which comprises the balance of this ersatz land of dreams.

At the west end of the island, beyond the small stockade-enclosed zoo, there is a vast green meadow surrounded on all sides by tall trees, mostly white birch, and spotted by only occasional small clumps of those same trees within its confines. Neither the river nor the opposite shores show through the natural privacy fence provided by the birches, almost creating the impression that there is no world beyond this, that the domed sky above encloses this emerald lawn as God's private preserve. The only sign of man's incursion, at the far west end of the meadow, is an old British blockhouse, now fallen into ruin, a remnant of the abortive American attempts during the War of 1812 to invade Canada. Even this relic of a war long past, its wood long ago silvered and mossed by the passing seasons, now seems only part of the landscape. Leaving the hustle bustle of the nineteenth century amusement park behind them, Steve and Janice spend their afternoon secluded in what seems an infinitely older yet more ageless world, a world that seems made for them alone, their privacy interrupted only by an occasional other couple passing across the green or by the tiny island train in the distance, its twin line of rails describing the perimeter of their world.

Late in the day they have their picnic lunch in the shadow of the old blockhouse, enjoying the birdsong and squirrel chatter that occasionally breaks their isolation. Then they walk again until they have explored even the furthest reaches of their little park. Finally, sated, they walk back in the glow of the setting sun toward the small boat that will carry them to the car. Once or twice Janice imagines she sees the young mime and she thinks to offer him a ride, but he always fades into the crowd before she has a chance to approach him.

93

Chapter Thirty

Steve and Janice relax together Sunday and he drives her home in time to dress and drive to work Monday morning. He has only just arrived back home when the telephone rings.

"Good morning."

"Hello. It's me. No names, okay."

"I understand. What's up."

"I have some more information. Also, the system for contacts."

"You want to meet?"

"Right."

"You sound strange. Are you at work?"

"Right."

"Do you want to meet the same place as last time?"

"No. The other place is all right."

"When?"

"Same time as before. Next three days. I'll get you one time."

"Starting today?"

"Yes."

"Okay, if there's nothing else...."

"I'll talk to you later."

***

Peter Goodman does not show up until nearly four o'clock on Wednesday afternoon, although Steve has been at the Shenendoah each day before three and has waited. He is growing impatient when he finally hears the familiar voice.

"Hi. I got here the soonest I could."

"I've been waiting since Monday. What's happening?"

"You hear about Peterson?"

"Wino? Yes, saw it in the paper. Last Friday."

"Murder. Guess that shows what we're up against."

"Yeah."

"There's more. I think Lazlo or somebody must have been after Atracura. The last few days there have been meetings all over town, Lazlo's people and Atracura's. Either something big is about to happen or else they are onto those guys from Ottawa. Or maybe..."

"...Maybe we really do have a problem."

"Right. You've been asking a lot of questions. Maybe it's us, or at least you, they're worried about."

"Let's hope not; keep our fingers crossed."

"More than that. We have to be more careful. I'm worried about it all: the Lazlo bunch, Atracura, the mystery boys from Ottawa, the department covering up. I can't call you any more. Don't you try to call me."

"You said. So how do we meet? What if I learn something? Or you do?"

"We'll use the paper."

"What?"

"Listen, I've figured it out. A simple code, and the classified ads. That's all we need."

"What? You mean pass on information through the paper?"

"No. Just meetings. You know: day, place, time, only what is really necessary. We can put it in the personals. All we need is to agree on a few choice words and the rest can be a love message or whatever."

"What do you mean, a few choice words?"

"Well, like this place could be 'the old place' maybe, and the corner on Highway 3 could just be 'out of town'. Then we'll need names for each of us...."

"You mean like 'Lance' and 'Fuzzy'?"

"That's the idea!"

"I don't know. It all seems like some kids game, or something from a bad movie. What if it doesn't work? How many of these code words are we going to need?"

"It's gotta work--unless you have a better suggestion?"

"Not now, I don't."

"Listen, I think if we have the locations and names, we can fake the rest. To be safe we should just set up meetings anyway. We can pass on any information in person."

"Okay: personals, 'Lance,' 'Fuzzy,' 'old place,' 'out of town.' Right?"

"It'll have to do."

"You sure you don't mind 'Fuzzy?' I was just joking when I said it."

"It'll do. Just read the personals every day. I'll be in touch. If you need me, take an ad. Remember, no telephones unless it's life or death."

Steve Lansing is again alone in the flickering half light of the Shenendoah Tavern, his eyes focused on the rainbow hues dancing on the bubbles of his half finished beer in reflection of the onstage floods that play across the sinuous body of the black girl, Hyacinth, as she dances across the small stage. As her set ends, the flood lights turning her warm, earthy colouring a cool blue shade, Steve finishes his beer and leaves.

Chapter Thirty One

Like a Swiss clockwork mechanism triggered by an electronic dial tone from French Canada, an intricate organization shifts into action, each piece in turn moving as it is prompted by the one before. In his luxurious Dearborn offices, Frank Lazlo presses the button to shut off the speaker phone on his desk, then turns to Rudy Noiraud.

"You heard."

"Yes, I heard. Tonight."

"Get on it."

"I will."

"No problems this time."

"I'll take care of it."

Rudy walks out of the office, leaving his employer looking from the twenty fourth floor windows across the black void toward the blue glow above what must be downtown Detroit and Windsor beyond. At eleven o'clock, Bud Atracura receives a call at his home from a pay telephone somewhere in Dearborn. The message is brief. Moments later he leaves the air conditioned comfort of his South Windsor residence for the untapped privacy of a shopping centre pay phone, then he drives to the Windsor Taxi Company garages on University Avenue, where he meets one of his drivers, who takes over dispatch from the man who has been on duty. Nearly two hours later, the telephone rings. Instead of the usual calls for a taxi or to ask the time, there are only four words said before the telephone is hung up.

"Rudy. Half an hour."

This time, Bud Atracura is taking no chances. He knows that another mistake might be more than he can afford. He speaks briefly with his man in the dispatch booth, then he gets into one of the blue and yellow cabs that he owns, and drives into the humid Windsor night.

Rudy Noiraud is driving too. This time he is alone in the black Cadillac Seville, rolling through the nearly empty freeways to Detroit and into what could be the shadow of the Renaissance Center were it not for the diffusion of blue streetlight and rainbow neon filling the night air. Although it is slightly further from Dearborn than the bridge would be, Rudy has chosen the tunnel beneath the Detroit River as his route to Windsor, a precaution against being associated with the other car. He pays the toll, then rolls into the eternal fluorescence of the tunnel, gliding the Cadillac between the white ceramic walls toward Canada. When he has cleared the Canadian Customs, he drives quickly to the Windsor Taxi Company garages, where the door opens quickly to admit his car then closes as quickly behind him.

The man who is operating the dispatch office explains, between calls, why Mr. Atracura is not present to meet Mr. Noiraud. Mr. Noiraud smiles. He seems, at least to the taxi driver, to approve. The driver returns to his telephones and his radio. Rudy Noiraud sits in the Cadillac to wait.

In the blue glow that nearly lights the fifth floor of the municipal parking garage, a sleek red and white antique car purrs in anticipation of an imminent visitor. Within moments a blue and yellow Windsor Taxi slinks quietly up the ramp and into position beside the Crown Victoria. Lucio Atracura turns off his motor and steps out of the cab. He is alone, but the old car's motor is running. He waits. He is still waiting ten minutes later, and he is growing impatient. He starts to get back into the cab. As he does so, one of the shadows against the pillars behind him forms itself into the shape of a man, moving slowly and quietly behind him.

When he revives, his head aching from a blow, he sees that the bulky brown envelope that had been laying on the passenger's side of the front seat is gone, or rather, miraculously transformed into a brown paper wrapped box about two feet square. Looking around, he sees that the old Ford has gone. He is alone in the half

dark of the parking garage. Beside him on the seat is his wallet. He
checks. The money is all there. The accordion section for credit
cards and identification is pulled open. Bud understands. With some
pain he manages to sit up in the driver's seat but it takes him several
minutes before he feels capable of driving. Then he returns to the
company garage, to his appointment with Rudy Noiraud.

***

It has been a good party night for a Thursday. Jane Lesley
and Trixie LaBelle have made the best of it, between the few drinks
they have bought themselves and the drinks that have been bought
for them in a forgotten number of bars. It has been a grand night to
party but last call has come and gone and the celebrants must either
find a private party or find their way home.

Usually, Jane and Trixie have no trouble finding a couple of
gallant gentlemen to drive them home after a night of partying, but
tonight, while the partying has been excellent, the rides have been
sparse. Having failed to cadge a ride from a barroom companion, the
two celebrants decide to try hitching a ride on the open road rather
than pay taxi fare. Now they are in the midst of an unconsciously
choreographed schottische in slow motion along University Avenue
toward downtown Windsor, pausing periodically to face in the
direction from which they have come, thumbs stuck upward in the
night air and bodies swaying gracefully like marsh grass in the wind.
The few cars pass without so much as a flicker of brake light and the
weaving, whirling, waltzing down University Avenue continues in the
blue haze of early morning mist and street lights.

"C'mon. Let's cross the street."
"Trix, we gotta go home."
"Come."
"Don' pull me! You nuts or somethin'?"
"'s a ride."
"Wrong way, Trix. I'm not that drunk. Stop pulling me!"
"C'mon. It's Steve."
"What Steve? 's no one there!"
"Not there, silly. Down the street, coupla."
"What?"

"Couple blocks, red light. That's Steve's car, eh?"

"Hey! You're right!"

"I know."

Following the tortuous route mapped by their only semi-piloted feet, the two women manage to gain a position on the opposite side of the road and resume their swaying stance beside the curb, arms extended toward the traffic lanes. The lights have changed from green to yellow to red and the expected car is on its way toward them. As it nears the two figures at the roadside, their stance shifts to a synchronous leaning out and waving of hands reminiscent of some overdone vaudeville exit. The red and white car flies by as though the two waving forms were only will of the wisp and turns several blocks further down, into the entrance ramp for the Ambassador Bridge.

"Trix?"

"I know. Fuck, is Steve Lansing ever go'n hear from me! He mus' have some hot date over there."

Chapter Thirty Two

The world of Rudy Noiraud is a comfortable one this morning. He has done his job well. The meeting last night went as smoothly as could ever be expected. Now he is wrapped in the softness of his woman, drifting in that nearer netherland that lies somewhere between dreams and reality. He is not really eager to wake, but the gentle enticements of Lise Martin arouse his interest in the world outside his head: first in the coital comforts of the house he helps finance in substantial degree, and then in the job he began last night but has not completed, will not complete until later this morning. In fact, Rudy is supposed to have secreted himself in a hotel or motel somewhere in town, a place he will not be known or remembered, but Lise is special and the box is as safe in her home as in a motel. While part of Rudy tells him that this is a secret rendezvous, he does not really fool himself that anything has been put over on Frank Lazlo. He has worked long enough and closely enough with his employer to know that there is nothing that is kept from his attention for long. Still, if Frank knows about Rudy's regular visits to this other home in Windsor, he has never mentioned the illicit stops on delivery days. Rudy takes this as a sign of acquiescence, a minor foible allowed for many jobs well done.

By nine thirty, Rudy is up, bathed, dressed, and driving his Cadillac toward another sort of rendezvous several miles away at the Humble Gas Bar near Highway 401. He eases the black car into a space on the tarmac near where the large tractor trailer units are parked, several hundred feet from the building itself. He locks the car and walks to the restaurant. At this time of the morning only a few tables are occupied. Rudy stops and scans the faces in the restaurant before he enters. At the long counter only one seat is taken, by one of the gas bar's mechanics taking a coffee break. Four men, apparently truckers aged in a range from twenty five to forty, congregate around one of the more central tables. A middle aged couple who have the look of American tourists has chosen a table by the window, although the only view is the spreading tarmac and the endless miles of half grown corn fields beyond. Two business suited men in their late twenties, probably travelling salesmen he thinks, have the only other occupied table. He selects a table in the shaded part of the room and sits down facing the large windows that run the length of the south wall. He orders coffee, and he waits.

***

Across the restaurant dining room from Rudy Noiraud, the black looks of concentration exchanged by the two men in business suits do not reflect concern over the sales of ball bearings or vacuum cleaners but consternation over the movements of a certain red and white automobile. By the time Rudy had arrived at the Humble Gas Bar, Frank Teufel and Les Malenfant had been talking across their coffee for more than an hour. They have heard this morning that the American car was seen in Windsor last night. This upsets them because they should have known in advance if there was a delivery being made. It upsets them because they are working in a vacuum. They are aware that Commander Pazitch has a number of people, individuals and small groups of two or three, working in Detroit and Windsor, yet they have been kept in ignorance of who these others are or even of their exact numbers. It is one of these people who has informed Ottawa that the car has been in town.

Nominally, Frank Teufel is in charge of the south western Ontario operation. Les Malenfant is his second in command. Yet they must make all requests for materials or manpower through head office, and they receive all information back from the same source. In reality, they are alone in Windsor, with no idea who is with or who against them. They are different only in that they have the direct telephone number for the Commander; the others, as far as Frank and Les know, have only the callback number, an automatic telephone that takes messages by tape recorder. Today this system especially irks. A direct call from a local subordinate would have put them on the yankee's trail in a few minutes. The recorded message in the nation's capitol was not picked up and relayed back to Windsor until several hours later. Les is furious. Frank is more chagrined, but he knows there is little that can be done about the system. For Commander Pazitch, security is more important than efficiency. He has placed several people in sensitive positions in both the border cities and, so long as they do not know who their partners are, they cannot talk if they are found out and captured. All Frank Teufel can expect is a modicum of additional information: the Commander's direct number, code names and approximate capabilities of several of the local operatives, and collation of information gathered by all the people in his group. The Commander will not allow more than that. All Frank can do is commiserate with Les on the difficulty of working within an imperfect system. Neither man is satisfied. They have a difficult job to do, and their own people are erecting barriers in their path.

"We could have stopped him."

"I know, Les. Shit! I know."

"He probably made another drop. Another shipment to God knows where!"

"Can't be helped now. We'll get the bastard next time! Next time."

"If the whole system doesn't fuck us up! Damn them! We coulda fucking had him!"

"We'll get him. Our way."

"What's that supposed to mean?"

"It means the system doesn't work. It means we're on our own, made that way by the Commander. Okay, we will take all the info we can get from his other people here, and from Ottawa too. But we'll go after it more on our own."

"There's nothing to go after. What have we got?"

"Lansing. The taxi company, especially Atracura. That Wino guy who died. We'll start asking some of our own questions, get our own operatives."

"That takes money, time."

"Time! Shit, we've got nothing but time right now! And there's our contingency allotment for expenses: we haven't even begun to touch that! I'm going to start hitting the Commander for that money. He'll come through."

"Just so we get the fucking yankee!"

"We will. We will."

During their time at the truck stop this morning, much of their conversation has run in circles, making clear that what had begun as just another assignment has become, through the frustrations posed by their own organization and the one against which they are pitted, a bitter personal vendetta by Malenfant and to a lesser degree by Teufel against an unknown American. Irresolution born of their discontent has kept them hunched over coffee rather than parked across from 321 Riverside Drive East. Finally, sometime after ten thirty, they rise from their chrome chairs to commence the day's work.

***

His second cup of coffee has stopped in mid-passage between saucer and mouth as Rudy gazes intently across the hot black asphalt toward the Cadillac. An older model Freightliner tractor, equipped with a sleeper behind the cab and a wind deflector on the roof, its deep grey paint a complement to the silver of the trailer it is hauling, has pulled into the lot and is parking next to the car. The driver, a blond man in his mid-twenties, gets out and walks to the restaurant. After a brief pause in the doorway, he joins Rudy at the table and orders coffee. They do not discuss business.

The box moves from the trunk of the Seville to the sleeper of the tractor. The grey transport truck moves into the flow of traffic on the 401 toward Toronto, Montreal, and beyond. The black Cadillac moves into the opposite stream, seeking the serpentine arch of the Ambassador Bridge. Not far behind, two men uncomprehendingly follow in a dark blue Buick Regal. The sun has not yet begun to move downward.

***

Steve Lansing has risen early for a Friday morning, thanks to a nine o'clock telephone call from his friend Trixie LaBelle remonstrating with him for deserting his friends in the dark of night. Apparently she has again seen him where he was not. A walk downtown brings comments from several of his street people friends that he has bypassed them as well the previous evening. Now, nearly two hours after the telephone dragged him rudely into the world, after he has made apologies and tried to explain that his car was home all night, Steve is walking through the double glass doors of *The Star* with a typewritten message for the personals column. He hands the receptionist in Classified Advertising the slip of paper along with a crinkled blue five dollar bill and waits for his change. The ad will not appear until Saturday's paper, so all he can do is wait.

***

As though he has stood in suspended animation overnight, Frank Lazlo stands behind the grey tinted picture windows of his twenty fourth floor office looking across the sunlit cityscape toward the backside of the Detroit skyline. He is thoughtful as his second in command enters the air-conditioned opulence of carpet, wood, and steel that is headquarters for Lazlo Associates, a Michigan corporation ostensibly involved in consulting, although the specific field of consultation is anybody's guess, through which moves a constant stream of monies of indeterminate origin and uncertain destination, leaving behind a considerable residue of consulting fees for Frank Lazlo. Rudy Noiraud softly closes the door behind himself and crosses the room, standing a short distance behind the static figure of his employer.

"Is it done?"

"It's probably in Toronto by now."

"Good."

"Atracura picked it up himself."

"What? Why?"

"I guess he didn't want to take a chance on another driver screwing up. I don't know."

"Anybody else involved?"

"Just a driver watching dispatch. Seems all right."

"And it all went okay?"

"Like clockwork."

"Good. We'll be doing it again real soon."

"When?"

"I'm not sure. I'll let you know."

"You need anything else from me now? Otherwise I'll take off for the weekend."

"Nothing now. Enjoy your weekend, just let me know where I can reach you. I've heard some rumblings from over the border that worry me, may need to talk to you if I hear more."

"I'll keep the pager on."

"Good. You going to Canada?"

"I might."

Frank Lazlo nods a gentle dismissal and Rudy Noiraud passes out of the cool, shady office down to the street level Detroit summer.

Chapter Thirty Three

In the first flush of morning the grey and silver transport truck descends through the rush of traffic, from the Macdonald-Cartier Freeway ever lower through the connecting stream of flowing steel and glass and finally into an older industrial district on the northwest corner of Montreal. Several streetcorners later the truck wheels into the empty loading area of an old brick warehouse, manoeuvres into position facing the gate through which it has just entered, and stops. The driver steps tentatively down from the cab, then seeing no one else around walks exploratively around the high fenced lot as he waits.

Jimmy Dolan is an American. He has lived in Canada since the sixties, using draft evasion as his excuse to emigrate from his native Missouri, although he had the added incentive of several state issued warrants for his arrest. Since arriving in Canada he has maintained a low profile, working in construction and driving for various trucking firms, finally buying his own second hand tractor and trailer about three years ago. To supplement his income, Dolan has frequently done favours for contacts he has who work outside the normal constraints of society. What he has done, Dolan has done well, avoiding the handicap of a Canadian criminal record while enhancing his own value to those who would employ his services.

It is nearly an hour before a new black Buick rolls through the open gate and stops beside the parked truck. Dolan, who has beensitting on some lumber near the fence smoking a cigarette, walks over to the car as two men in dark business suits step out. What little conversation passes between the parties betrays enough accent to tell Jimmy Dolan that these men are Americans, one from New York and the other from Texas or possibly Oklahoma. His practiced face does not reveal his surprise that the contacts are not Canadian. He transfers the package from the cab of his tractor to the trunk of the car and accepts the bulky envelope that fulfils the fee already half paid by Rudy Noiraud in Windsor, counting the bundled tens and twenties before climbing back up to his driver's seat. The black car leaves, followed shortly by the highway transport.

Under the burning midday sun, Dolan feels that dark magnetism which any large city has for large amounts of cash, especially if ill gotten, his newly harvested lucre pulling him irrevocably toward that glittering marketplace of dreams which is Montreal's core. He spends the afternoon finding a place to park his rig, buying complete new clothing, registering and bathing, then leaves his room for dinner and an evening on the town. After a circuit of Montreal's best downtown clubs and bars, and some not so fine, he continues his private celebration in his sky high room at the luxurious Chateau Champlain in company with the young lady who will share his bed until daylight.

As morning's light deflects from the shining tower of the Chateau Champlain, the truck driver sits in the shade of his room, a stack of brown and purple bills on the writing desk before him. A quick accounting tells him that he has hardly scratched the surface of his new hoard. Windsor seems a long way off.

Shower, shave, dress: within half an hour Jimmy Dolan is descending the hotel's elevator to that fluorescent netherworld which underlies the streets of Montreal, a labyrinth of shops, restaurants and myriad delights where he will remain until he surfaces to the temptations of the cosmopolitan nightlife. Not until Saturday will he emerge, the grey and silver transport following the highway westward.

***

Monday in Detroit's summer heat is less blue than grey, the humid haze veiling the sky and screening the sun, which nevertheless persistently pours its fire down on the steaming city. Rudy Noiraud sits in the faint shadow of an awning on the front of the Hotel

Ponchartrain, enjoying the slight breeze as it plays across tables with the illusion of a cooling effect. He sits peevishly with a Michelob half poured into his glass, facing but not really looking at Cobo Hall and, beyond that, Canada across the Detroit River. Frank Lazlo will soon expect him to report and he has heard nothing from Montreal. Having nothing to report can be risky, even for someone as well established and highly ranked as Rudy.

Rudy is jolted from his introspection by the regular beeping from the box on the table beside his beer. Turning the switch off, he walks quickly into the hotel lobby, where he calls his answering service on a pay telephone. The message is from Montreal, concise and to the point:

Arrived safely. Thanks.

Rudy drops in more coins and dials again. When the Dearborn number answers, he asks for Frank Lazlo. When the extension is picked up moments later, nobody speaks.

"Frank? Is that you?"

"Rudy. I was waiting to hear from you."

"They have the package."

"Good."

"Is there anything else you need tonight?"

"No. But I have to talk to you. Tomorrow. First thing."

"Okay, about nine?"

"That's good. Meet me here, downstairs in the lobby."

"What's it about, Frank?"

"I can't say now. We'll talk tomorrow."

"Okay, Frank. I'll see you then."

Rudy hangs up the telephone and walks across the lobby, back to the outdoor patio where his unfinished beer still sits in the shade. While he has been on the telephone a street entertainer, a young mime he has seen from time to time in Windsor, has come and is performing for the patio's patrons. He moves from table to table, coins and eggs appearing and disappearing in his hands, ears, and mouth plus various cups and other containers on the patio tables. By the time he arrives at Rudy's table, he has in his hands something new, an antique jewellery box, shaped like a treasure chest. He demonstrates that it is empty and closes the lid, then draws from the chest a long, rainbow hued handkerchief which vanishes, apparently into thin air. When he next opens the chest, it is filled with gold coins. About this time several raindrops find Rudy's table and he notices that the sky has darkened in anticipation of an early summer cloudburst. Rudy finishes his beer quickly and leaves. The entertainer has already vanished somewhere along Jefferson Avenue.

Almost as soon as Rudy Noiraud reaches his car the storm breaks with primeval ferocity, inundating the earth and filling the skies with sheets of fire. Forces other than man have taken the city as their own.

Chapter Thirty Four

> **FUZZY,** please meet me same time the old place.
> Monday if possible or I'll wait. It's important I see
> you. Lance.

During his afternoon coffee break in the police station cafeteria, Staff Sergeant Peter Goodman has been reading the weekend edition of The Star, paying particular attention to the personals section of the classified advertisements. Seeing the ad he has been waiting for, he sets the paper aside. The timing is ideal. If the ad had not appeared today, he would have gone Monday and placed his own message in the personals in the hope of a meeting later in the week. Now there is no need. He is working today and tomorrow but off both Monday and Thursday, so the meeting will be no problem. He picks up the national magazine section of the paper and continues reading until his break is over.

***

Monday moves slowly for Steve. His weekend lethargy has carried over, leaving him with little inclination to work, so that he spends the time partially reading but mostly sitting looking across the river at the Detroit skyline framed by his apartment's bay window.

Around lunchtime he makes a peanut butter sandwich to supplement the coffee he has been drinking all morning. What starts out to be a brief catnap in the afternoon sun that streams in his window turns into an extended sleep from which he does not return until after two thirty. Rousing himself, he dresses and walks to the dank confines of the Shenendoah Tavern, arriving only shortly before three. Wondering if his message has been received, he sits down to wait. At three ten, Peter Goodman approaches him through the dimly lit cigarette haze and sits down.

"I saw the ad."

"I notice."

"Actually, I was going to run a message for you. You beat me to it."

"You got something new?"

"Tell me what you got first. I'll take it from there."

"All right. The car was in town. Thursday night. Quite a few people saw it, thought it was me. And another thing, one of my friends saw it going onto the bridge. Maybe it's an American, eh? Maybe that's why he disappears so quick."

"That's it?"

"I thought it might be important."

"Maybe. It seems to fit. A friend of mine on customs at the tunnel says Rudy Noiraud—he's Lazlo's number two hand—came over Thursday night, late. He never went back while my friend was working, unless he used the bridge."

"So what's the connection?"

"I don't know. But if that Vicky is an American car...."

"Then what? What does this, uh, Rudy, have to do with it?"

"Maybe nothing. But it's worth checking. After all, Lazlo is somehow connected with the two guys from Ottawa, and they seem to be after that car."

"Uh huh."

"And I've done some more checking with the computer, just feeding in what we already have, changing the combination of information."

"And...?"

"Teufel and Malenfant may not be on their own down here. We've been getting a series of numerical codes that seem to designate personnel, maybe as many as a dozen, but we still can't figure which agency they work for. That American key keeps showing up, almost every time, so my friend is trying it on the computers he knows of in the states. It would help if we knew which one it is, but we may still get lucky."

"What else?"

"Not much. I've been putting out feelers. It seems that Atracura has a habit once in a while of leaving home late at night for several hours, and there are a couple of pay phones he uses a lot. If I can find a way, I'll try to get them tapped. He must have a reason for not using his home or office phones. That's about it."

"So where does that leave us? Anywhere?"

"Well, if you're right about the car being from the states, it looks more and more like we're dealing with yankees. Other than that, we don't really know anything more than before."

"Yeah."

"I'll be in touch."

"Okay. By the way...."

"What?"

"The ad worked good. You want to stay with that system?"

"What else?"

When the policeman has faded into the half light and out the door, Steve signals Marj for another beer and settles back to watch one more set before returning to his apartment. Several sets later, when Steve finally forsakes the swaying, swirling rainbow lit female form writhing in the dingy bar, the sun is already setting. Steve walks slowly home in the greying day, the Detroit skyline ahead of him on Ouellette Avenue assumed or silhouetted in the fire of a subsiding summer afternoon.

Once home, Steve settles almost immediately into a sleep that will last until morning. Janice has taken on an extra job at work and will remain at home tonight to complete the task.

***

After a fourteen hour day, Janice Bergeron is tired. A listless weekend has meant a backlog of work for Monday and Janice has not stopped, even for lunch, finishing the routine office tasks early and

113

plunging immediately into completion of the special proposal she has agreed to plan and assemble for Mr. Jackson, her employer. With the project now well under way, she is ready for a good night's sleep. She has been so occupied that she only now remembers that Steve was to have met with Peter Goodman this afternoon. Had she remembered earlier, she would have called him, gone to his apartment to find out what happened. Now, rather than take a chance on discussing it on the telephone, she will wait until morning and have breakfast downtown. Steve can tell her then about the meeting. She sets the alarm back half an hour to allow time for breakfast. Sleep comes quickly and easily.

Outside it has been raining for several hours off and on and the repressive black of Ontario's summer night has flowed across the sodden land, filling every available opening with an almost tangible inkiness that even the fire that periodically seizes control of the sky cannot dispel. The second storey bedroom of the townhouse is no exception in this dank, muggy humidity and in its dusky, cloying blackness. The blackest of the shadows seems to reach out, grasping Janice and ripping her to a seated position as she awakes to the sound of an explosive crash and a woman's scream.

It takes her a few shocked seconds to reach out and turn on the bedside lamp. As the light reclaims the room, driving the darkness out the open window, Janice slowly reconnoitres the normality of her room and realizes the explosion must have been thunder, the screams her own. By morning Janice will have awakened several times, each as suddenly as the first time. She is again having the terrifying, realistic dreams which have plagued her since childhood. She spends most of the night in the protective brilliance of the bedside lamp, left on to fend off the dark spirits of the night.

Chapter Thirty Five

Taller than a man by half, and gently flicking and waving on all sides of her like ever so many benign red and yellow cattail leaves, the flames seem to mean Janice no harm as she walks in comfort among them, but suddenly they snap and they snarl and they crackle with a violence she has not noticed before this. She begins to feel heat, intensifying heat that soon achieves unbearable proportion. Her clothes explode into flames leaving her writhing and screaming in this demonic garden.

Janice is awake. But she is not at home and it takes her a while to realize where she is sitting. She is at Steve's apartment, seated now on the chesterfield where she had a while ago been sleeping, with the morning sun filling the bay window with light. At the centre of the living room there is a snake, a hooded snake with a long curled up body, like a cobra she saw in a movie once. It is a minor revelation to Janice, who cannot recall Steve ever expressing interest in this sort of plaster kitsch. She turns her head for only a second to look out the bay window, and when she turns back to the room the snake seems larger somehow.

It is larger. And it is growing! Soon it has almost filled the room with its expanding serpentine bulk, a great silver snake with a grey hooded head, leering down hungrily at her with its fiery eyes and darting tongue. Horrified, she again turns her head toward the bay window, this time with her arms flung upward in a vain effort to ward off what seems certain doom. Like some berserk kamikaze comet, the flaming ball of the sun has flown across the top of the towering silver Renaissance Center and is headed directly toward the apartment—toward Janice who no longer knows where to look! The sun bursts through the bay window in a shower of shattered glass, splintered wood, and rainbow hues and falls to the floor in front of the serpent, a four foot ball of flames.

Blinded and transfixed by the initial brilliance of the fiery orb, as though peering at the centre of a floodlight bulb, Janice regains progressively portions of her sight, firstly in flashes of colour, then in shadowy forms and finally something approaching normality. With her eyes hopelessly locked on the spectacle before her, she sees the dragonesque silver form behind the sun transmogrify, at first only to a shadowy wraith but gradually to a recognizable human shape, a man with longish blond hair, his features obscured by the heat wave distortion of the sun. As though following the earlier example of the silver snake, the sun begins to expand, burgeoning and ballooning like a newsreel A-bomb threatening to fill and surpass the space within the room. In a futile attempt to quell the growing gorgon flames around the glowing ball, the now hominid snake throws himself over the new arrival in a spreadeagle of ineffective grasping. The man could be Steve. Janice is not sure.

Her peripheral vision is caught by another movement, pulling her head to the right. In the shell that was the bay window crouches a slender man in coveralls with a small black hat and a white face. From his eyes flow black, inky tears that fall noiselessly to the window ledge and run from there along the plaster wall to make a pool of black on the floor. His mouth, really only a thin line loop of black lip, is going through the motions of speech, although nothing is audible and he seems to become increasingly angry—at himself or at her—because she cannot hear what he is trying to say. Finally, as though gripped by the utterest frustration, he beckons once, then again, and when she does not move toward him he reaches out, grabbing her arm and pulling her from the chesterfield toward the unwindowed frame he crouches in. She is more amazed than scared at his sudden action, for the sensation is that of floating through the air toward the window, and the sight of the mime's arm suddenly elastic and stretching nearly five feet to grasp hers before retracting seems giddily fantastic. She is beginning to laugh by the time her body floats into that of the white faced man and they both tumble through the open window frame. A quick glance over her shoulder reveals the solar battle continuing, with a would-be Prometheus failing to harness a sun that grows ever larger and brighter until it must sooner rather than later fill the room with light and flames. Then she is sailing in slow motion—like a David Lean love scene or some Peckinpah explosion, she thinks as she watches herself floating down—executing a graceful arc in parallel to the one described by the falling form of the mime toward the street below.

As Janice stands on Riverside Drive with the mime, she remembers that the man inside may be Steve, may be in terrible danger, may need help only she can give. As she starts toward the building the mime seems to read her thoughts and steps into her path, blocking her way again as she attempts to step around. Ire and panic combine in Janice to give her the strength to push the white faced man to the ground, but before she can rush past him toward the apartment he changes. Rising toward her is the face of a great cat, a great golden lion growling at her and forcing her back from his glowing face, a face now not so much that of the lion as that of some oriental glowing sun. The terror in Janice is too much, and when the expanding lionsunface explodes her whole being explodes with it, becoming an atomic scream that echoes through the world.

The exploding roar and the redounding scream echoing through her head, Janice sits bolt upright in her bed. The terror of the darkness only half allowing her to believe it is only thunder and her own voice crying out in the night. She reaches for the bedside lamp.

Chapter Thirty Six

The knocking will not stop. The persistent battering of the apartment door continues, battering as well the walls of Steve's comfortable retreat, gradually weakening defences so that he knows he must awaken. Rolling over and rising on one elbow, he looks at the alarm clock beside the bed. It is only eight o'clock. He wonders who could be calling on him at such an unreasonable hour. By now parts of him are coming awake, so he drops his feet to the floor and, after a quick shove against the bed, allows his body to rise into position above them. His head is still a bit hazy as he grabs his robe from the chair it is usually thrown across and wraps it around his body on his way to the door.

Outside the door, standing in the small entrance hall, he finds Janice, her face betraying that all is not well. Inviting her in, he offers coffee and some breakfast, which she is quick to accept. Now that he is more awake, Steve has Janice sit on the chesterfield while he prepares breakfast: coffee first, then bacon and eggs. They will talk after they have eaten. While he is cooking, Steve tries to appear as bright and cheerful as possible to buoy Janice's spirits, and he tries to puzzle out what could upset her enough to come over unannounced yet forget her key to the apartment. At the door she has mentioned a dream, but there must be more to it, something additional to so panic her.

Steve's performance as chef has worked its magic and Janice brightens a bit during breakfast, but there is still a cloud of concern behind her eyes and twitching at the corners of her mouth. Breakfast is peaceful but brief. After breakfast Janice insists on first hearing about the meeting with Peter Goodman. Steve gives her a precis version of the Monday afternoon meeting, touching on all the major points, then pressures her to tell him what has gotten her so upset. Janice tells him in detail a dream she has dreamt so many times that she knows it by rote. She worries out loud that the dream may come true, that something strange may happen here in Steve's apartment. When Steve disallows this notion as fantasy, Janice points out that many of her dreams seem to come true.

"That's just the point. Janice, they only seem to come true. You dream things that partly come out of your real life, then you take the other parts, the parts that don't seem to make much sense, and you bend them like some intellectual craftsman to fit events that happen afterward. Your mind changes the memory of the dream to suit the event you think it foretells. Can't you see that?"

"No. I don't think so."

"Well, look at last night. You think your dream means some kind of trouble, but what does it really mean? You saw a blond guy in my place, but with long hair when mine was cut a couple of weeks ago. And that mime character: take away the rubber arm and you've probably got him from the kid we picked up when we went to Bob-Lo. No great mystery there! And what about all this stuff with snakes and the sun, eh? Sounds more like a Greek myth to me—that's what these dreams are, your own private myths, nothing more! Come on, nothing's going to happen!"

"I don't know...."

"Besides, even if it was true, and it isn't, the most you could do is foretell things. You can't make them happen, so you can't do much to stop them."

"It's just that, well, I worry."

"I know."

Janice leaves for another day of work, while Steve imagines he has calmed her. The balance of the week will be peaceful for Steve and Janice. Janice will not dream or, if she does dream, will not remember. Life will settle into a seeming normalcy that cannot be more than slightly disturbed by the continuing presence in the railway yard or behind the Ford of a now familiar dark Blue Buick grown peripheral and integral to the life of Steve Lansing.

Chapter Thirty Seven

Seen from the 747 high above, Highway 401 seems literally aswarm with tankers and tandems, flatbeds and every conceivable fashion of truck, with only occasionally an automobile visible in the stream of six a.m. traffic. Chatham, only about sixty miles from the border, stands out as a more strongly textured patch among the cornfields below. Returning to half-hearted perusal of the Time his flight attendant has given him, the passenger from Montreal leans back in his seat by the window. In a short time the jet will land in Windsor.

***

Slipping the grey Freightliner with its unladen silver trailer through the seventy mile per hour flow of 401 traffic, Jimmy Dolan welcomes the sight of the Tilbury water tower rising over the horizon to signal him that he will be back in Windsor in less than forty five minutes. It has been a good week for Jimmy Dolan. After one very simple job, he has revelled for five days and nights in the underworld bacchanal that hides within the glittering chrysalis of Montreal. The job paid well: enough that the remaining money will allow him to live quite well for the next month or two in Windsor and Detroit. And the job went smoothly enough that Jimmy is certain he will be offered more work from the same source. No, thinks Jimmy Dolan as he watches the town of Tilbury recede in his side mirrors, it has not been only a good week, it has been an excellent week!

***

In the light of the rising sun the city of Windsor, almost as though to welcome the arrivals from Montreal, is dressing up for a party. The week-long International Freedom Festival is about to begin. Downtown Windsor is blocked off by barricades creating a temporary pedestrian mall brightened by bunting and festival flags. Every vacant lot has become a mini carnival with rides and concessions, while the large vacant area next to the art gallery has magically flourished into a full midway overnight.

By ten o'clock the streets are already thronging with workers and fun seekers under the summer sun's benevolent gaze. Street entertainers mingle with office workers and store clerks, teens and tots and middle aged couples, well heeled salesmen and downtown winos, undercover cops and casual unemployeds, a kaleidoscope of humanity's variety flowing the streets of Windsor. High school and university musicians, singly, in small bands, and in orchestras, are scattered along Ouellette Avenue and through the riverfront parks to play for the public. A young guitarist from Toronto, his instrument case open before him, is in the process of learning that Windsorites are not as fiscally free as the residents of the city he has just left. By the end of the day his case will not contain much more than the three twenty five cent pieces he has himself placed there as a hint to passers by. There is the birdman warbling his watery notes from first this location and then that, basking in the attention the bubbling birdsong nets him through the day. There are clowns and costume characters representing various organizations from Bob-Lo Island to a local realtor, making the mall a jungle of lions and bears and Bozos enough to delight any child. And there is the young mime in black leotards and white coveralls, moving easily among the crowds on Ouellette Avenue and along Riverside Drive, performing sleight of hand and playing at Marceau for any and all who will watch. He has just finished performing for a small group of adults and children near the most easterly barricades on Riverside Drive about a block from Steve Lansing's apartment, bowing so deeply and with such a flourish that the crown of his small black bowler nearly brushes the pavement. He fades into the crowd. reappearing a half block further west.

***

As they step from the doorway onto the sidewalk, Janice imagines that she sees the mime among the throng a block or so away, the mime of their Bob-Lo trip, the mime of her nightmare, but as quickly as her grip tightens on Steve's arm the whiteface seems to have dissolved into the mass of celebrants. She elects to say nothing to Steve. Some part of herself has already said to her what Steve would have said, that the mime is only that and nothing more, that talking to him will prove nothing but that. Although she still has lingering shades of the dreams dancing in her subconscious, she resolves to enjoy the weekend.

They spend the day and most of the evening just walking around the downtown area of Windsor, occasionally spending a dollar or two but mostly just enjoying the sights that abound at every street corner and along every sidewalk. They tour the regional arts and crafts displayed in booths along the riverfront: jewellery, macrame, paintings and even a local cartoonist taking time off from The Star to sketch passers by for a nominal fee. They sample the wares of a dozen ethnic food booths. They walk through the midway, testing their skill on several of the games but deciding to stay off the rather shaky looking rides. They watch several of the musical groups playing renditions of dixieland and big band swing with varying degrees of skill. Steve thinks the young guitarist plays and sings fairly well and throws two quarters into the guitar case.

At ten thirty it is getting dark and the streets are beginning to clear under the blue mercury vapour lights. Rather than visit the beer tents by the river, Steve and Janice decide to return to the apartment for a glass of wine and some late night television. The beer tent will wait until later in the week. All in all it has been an enjoyable summer day and Janice does not want to bother Steve with her omens, her silliness as he might call it. She has enjoyed the day immensely but it has seemed everywhere she looked there were lions, horrid stuffed teddybear lions looming from among the crowds, and always she saw never near and dissolving into the masses, the mime.

Janice thinks she could use that glass of wine.

Chapter Thirty Eight

Waves of rock and roll wash over the glut of topers packing the huge tent near the Detroit River. Movement is minimal in the crush of underage drinkers, middle aged men playing greying Romeo to twentyish freeriders, habitual partygoers, and tourists of all sorts, but a few mismatched couples still dance in a small space near the disc jockey. At a corner table, Jimmy Dolan sits with the buxom form he has persuaded to join him when he returns home. In fact, both Jimmy and the young lady are feeling quite mellow and have decided that, for tonight, home will be defined as a suite at the Viscount Hotel, some of the more luxurious accommodations in the city. While it is barely ten thirty, they decide it is time to leave the public party for a more intimate party of their own. Taking a sinuous route through the pack in the beer tent, Jimmy and Shelley (which is what she has given as her name) sway their way across the grass of the park toward the new Cadillac convertible on which he has just made a cash down payment, then they drive to the Viscount and, once in the privacy of their luxurious suite, order enough champagne to last the rest of the night. For the newly affluent Jimmy Dolan, life has become one unending celebration.

***

In a more modest room elsewhere in the Viscount Hotel, one of Dolan's countrymen thinks back on his busy day. Since his arrival early this morning, Lou Silvaggio has hardly stopped. Rudy Noiraud had picked him up promptly at the airport and driven him to

123

Dearborn, briefing him along the way. The meeting with Frank Lazlo had been quite productive and had taken most of the morning. Lunch was another meeting, with Lazlo, Noiraud, and some other Lazlo associates—really a public relations effort for Lazlo—in the air conditioned half light of Chuck Muir's seafood restaurant in the Hotel Ponchartrain. After lunch, he had come back to Canada with Rudy Noiraud for meetings with Lucio Atracura and some of his principals. Silvaggio is not overly impressed with Atracura. His organization is too loose, hardly an organization at all, more like a consortium of petty chiefs with a nominal but powerless head. And Atracura himself seems too flighty, too easily bent by the prevailing wind. Silvaggio is of the opinion that Bud Atracura must be replaced. He represents too great a risk. There seem to be too many people looking into his operation. After the meetings with the Windsorites, there was a late dinner meeting at Ye Olde Steak House, a fashionable Windsor restaurant, this time with just himself, Lazlo, and Noiraud present.

This was Silvaggio's meeting. He had expressed his concern about Atracura, his compliments on the efficiency of Noiraud and those who work with him, especially the messenger Dolan, his general satisfaction with the way deliveries have been handled. He had probed to find out how the box had crossed the border so easily, but expected and got no direct answer, was only told someone else was involved. Then they had discussed future business, the handling of the next and subsequent shipments to the group in Montreal. That being done, etiquette had demanded a modicum of socializing, in this case a brief circuit of some of the better night clubs in Windsor and Detroit. Pleading exhaustion from his trip and from a rigourous day's work, he had had Noiraud drive him to the hotel after about two hours, just enough to be polite.

Lou Silvaggio was back in his room by eleven o'clock. He is satisfied with the way the day has gone. Tomorrow he will leave Windsor.

***

Night has drawn its dark banner across the face of the city. The silence is pervasive, broken only by the hush of the flowing river and the whisper of the summer wind. No motion is reflected in the upturned mirror of the late night sky. Festivities have expired with the waning light. The drinkers have driven or taxied home with the irreversibility of last call. Occasional taxicabs seem anomalous to the bluelit streets, cruising furtively in and out of the pervasive shadows.

A single form moves through this pall, walking along Sandwich Street, an hour from downtown's last call and still a long way westward to go. Even after a full day and night afoot, this slender human form with the white face moves steadily and smoothly through the darkness. The lone figure of a tireless, immortal form walks through the world in which Janice Bergeron sleeps. Next to Steve she feels at peace.

Chapter Thirty Nine

"Alright! So tell me who, Rudy! Just tell me who, that's all I want to know! Who?"

"I don't know, Frank, I just don't know."

"I'm so careful. Who can I trust? You? That cabdriver Atracura? Just who can I rely on anymore?"

"Frank. Stay cool. We'll find out, okay."

"Listen, this office, my home, even the car: checked, full electronic screen for bugs weekly. And I never take my car anywhere sensitive. You know I'm not followed! It's gotta be someone inside!"

"I know, Frank. But getting paranoid won't help."

"Somebody at the top. The information is too good; it's coming from the top, not any joeboy runner!"

"Frank, cool down! Listen. I know it's not me. You know it's not you. If we trust each other, maybe we can trace the leak. And plug it. Permanent."

"Wait a minute. Are you saying you're not sure I'm not the one? What's that supposed to mean?"

"Well, you do have a good record of not getting put away when your associates do..."

"Are you saying I set them up, Rudy?"

"No, Frank. I'm just saying if you feel you can't trust me after all this time, then I have as much reason not to trust you."

"What's that mean?"

"What it means is until we find out who's leaking information it's you and me against the world. We have to trust each other. We have to, Frank."

Sunday had started well for Rudy Noiraud. He and Lise had lain in bed late, in defiance of the eager sunshine and the summer sounds of birds and scrambling children's voices filling the cool grey of the bedroom from outside. They had risen in time to attend the noon mass and then had driven downtown to walk through the nearly vacant Freedom Festival mall before returning home. The agenda for the rest of the day was simple enough: sit on the patio with a cold beer until late afternoon, have a barbequed meal of Alberta beef steak and local corn, then sit on the patio until the advent of night. The harsh cry of the pocket pager added a new item to the agenda: an urgent meeting with Frank Lazlo in Detroit. Frank, it seems, had connected various bits of information, some of which were familiar to Rudy, and charging them with his own very active survival instinct had come up with a conspiracy, or at the very least a high level betrayal. Frank was upset, livid in fact. Frank is still livid.

"Okay, Frank, just stay cool. I'll go over it again and let's see what we've really got. Okay?"

"Yeah. Talk."

"All right. First off, in order, we know this Lansing guy has been poking around a lot, asking questions. And we know he was nosing around even before his problem with the cops. So, what can he find out about in Windsor?"

"Atracura. Not much more."

"Right. So a week ago you tell me you think the cops are checking us out. The same guys that are following Lansing are also asking around town. But who are they really asking about? Us? Not on your life! It's our careless cabdriver again."

"So? Go on."

"Silvaggio comes to town. He's got some beefs. But he likes the way we work, likes our people. Atracura he thinks is sloppy. Maybe too sloppy."

"So what are you getting at? Someone is still feeding out information. We're still getting screwed by our own people!"

"Maybe not. Listen. So now you hear that they suspect that we are making shipments. You hear they may have tied you in. You hear they are on to Atracura. Okay. But what does that really mean?"

"Someone talked."

"Maybe. But most of the attention seems to be on Bud and his cabs. I figure if someone is talking, it's one of his people, not ours. If they are watching him all that closely, it would take just one cop with a good border connection to tie me in. You're not the only one that can add two plus two. I think it's Atracura that has the problem."

"Perhaps you're right. Anyway, if we eliminate that possibility, we'll know. What do you suggest."

"Let me talk to him.""Soon?"

"Tomorrow. First thing. I'll take care of it."

"Make sure you do."

"Listen, I gotta couple of steaks waiting. Have we finished for now?"

"Sure. Call me tomorrow."

Chapter Forty

As though to provide a suitable setting for the discussion between Frank Teufel and Les Malenfant at the Humble Gas Bar, the Monday morning sky is grey and hazy, without a trace of the sun behind the overcast. Commander Pazitch has been in touch from Ottawa, in person, telephoning Frank Teufel late Sunday night with disturbing news.

Somebody has been checking into the Windsor operation. There is some evidence that the files in both Ottawa and Toronto have been accessed more than once through the Windsor Police computers. The exact number of times the headquarters files have been entered is not known, but no access was authorized. It is also suspected that attempts have been made to access the continental information bank in the United States, although the intruder apparently does not know the location of the American computer.

Ottawa suspects it all has something to do with Steve Lansing, partially due to his recent association with a Staff Sergeant, Peter Goodman. Goodman, who could be able to requisition computer time, began having secret meetings with Lansing at about the same time as the information thefts began. As well, Goodman is known to have requested information on the Buick that Teufel and Malenfant are using. Commander Pazitch suggests that his two operatives find out for certain the degree of Lansing's involvement—then make sure that all enquiries into the Windsor operation are stopped.

Malenfant wonders if there is a more specific directive as to how these enquiries are to be stopped. Teufel wishes there were. He believes the Commander is simply abdicating responsibility, covering his own behind in case of mistakes, by leaving the decision to be made in Windsor.

As the blue Buick leaves the parking lot of the Humble Gas Bar and turns toward Windsor, a light rain is beginning to fall.

Chapter Forty One

It is nine o'clock in the morning and a light rain is beginning to fall as Lucio Atracura walks through the street level door and down a flight of stairs into the Niagara, a workingman's restaurant in downtown Windsor. Rudy Noiraud is already waiting for him in a booth tucked into the corner furthest from the door. He walks over and sits down, accepting the coffee Rudy has already ordered him. He can see that his American colleague is troubled by something, but he cannot understand what might be the problem. As far as he can see, everything has been going very well the past few months. Except for the minor problem having to do with Rick Bergeron, there have been no hitches. he sips on his coffee, waiting for Rudy to speak.

"Well, Bud, how are things going?"

"Good."

"No problems?"

"Everything is very smooth."

"Your people behaving?"

"What do you mean?"

"No more trouble like Bergeron or Wino?"

"Naw. That was just a fluke! You know, because of the cops' mistake with that Lansing guy."

"Lansing leaving you alone?"

"Looks like, yeah."

"Things are going good. Right, Bud?"

"What are you getting at, Rudy? Things are good. Why the long discussion, eh?"

"Bud, things are not good. Not at all."

"What do you mean, not good?"

"Frank is worried. Silvaggio thinks your organization is real sloppy. You don't watch over your people close enough. You don't know what they are doing."

"Is that all? I can fix that. I'm already checking more often, having more meetings."

"It looks like we're being checked out by a lot of people. Lansing, for one, is still nosing around, whether you know it or not. And he's got at least one city cop helping him. We don't know whether the cop's in it on his own or if the department has an interest in what Lansing is doing. For all we know, he may be undercover himself; all that fuss could have been to establish a cover story, a fake antagonism with the cops! Worse, it looks like some sort of federal agency is investigating too. We don't know yet who they are, but they seem to be using Lansing to lead the way, so hopefully they haven't done too much on their own. Those guys my men spotted following Lansing, they're cops, and they're starting to ask questions on their own. Right now it looks like everything stops at Lansing, and his research into you."

"And...and you want...?"

"Lansing. I want Lansing, stopped. That should stop everyone. After Lansing, the trail is cold."

"I don't know. If there's that much interest in Lansing, it might be a mistake."

"You won't handle it?"

"It's just that I don't think..."

"Fine! You just take care of your organizational problems. I'll handle the other problem. Remember, Frank wants all information leaks stopped. Now! Make sure your group is airtight."

"Okay, Rudy. Okay."

"By the way, do you keep a list of your key people? You know, so you can find them quick when you need them."

"Sure. It's in my safe at home. Nobody gets near it but me. I've got no leaks, Rudy."

"Good. Listen, I've got to get back to Dearborn. Take care of yourself, okay."

Bud Atracura sits quietly in the booth for a few minutes, then drives to his garage to think some more about what has been said, to be sure he understands completely what Rudy has been telling him.

Chapter Forty Two

As usual, Steve is already well established at the table by the time Peter Goodman arrives, today promptly at three o'clock. After the customary greetings and ordering of beer, plus confirmation that of the two Goodman is alone in having new information to add to their small pool, the conversation slips into Peter's hands.

Although there remain a few questions he would like to have answered, Peter Goodman is a much happier, less fearful man than he has been for these past few weeks. He now feels reasonably assured that there is no dark conspiracy but that he and Steve have simply been caught up in a legitimate investigation, one that has grown too important and is hitting too close to the mark for those forces involved to allow betrayal by early disclosure of the facts because of a mistake like the Pitt Street shooting. With some expansion upon the known information and some conjecture to fill in the remaining gaps, Peter has added his new information to their previous pool and constructed what he believes to be the true scenario:

There is a truckdriver, Jimmy Dolan. He has, for the past week or so, been passing counterfeit Canadian ten and twenty dollar bills, first in Montreal and then in Windsor and Detroit. Dolan has some sort of criminal past in the United States but, although he appears to hang around with the less desirable elements of society, has managed to avoid problems with Canadian police. It is a moot point whether he is staying within the law or is just very clever at covering his tracks. It seems that Dolan does not know the unreal nature of his money, since he is spending the bills quite openly and is using his own name while doing so. It is possible that someone who hired Dolan's truck has paid him off in bogus bills.

Dolan has been seen, but only occasionally, with Rudy Noiraud. Dolan has no known connection with Lucio Atracura or with any of his associates. Rudy Noiraud has been seen in Atracura's company. The counterfeit money is of very high quality, the sort of product Frank Lazlo might consider becoming involved with, if he felt it was quite safe.

As Peter Goodman sees it, the story is simple. There is a large international counterfeiting operation for which Frank Lazlo has been serving as a middleman. Atracura has been an agent for Lazlo in the same scheme. Somehow, police in Canada or in the United States must have come across this operation and set up an international task force to stem the stream of illicit cash into legitimate channels: possibly the Mounties and O.P.P. in Canada working with the American F.B.I. (that could explain the American computer code key).

Teufel and Malenfant—he is still not certain which force they belong to—are probably the primary investigators, central to the whole operation. If it was actually Teufel and Malenfant who had shot at Steve in error, then they would not want to jeopardise, to betray, their investigation through unwanted subsequent hearings, especially if they felt they were close to breaking the counterfeiting ring.

Steve's stubbornness in reporting the shooting raised problems, for both sides of the investigative equation. Teufel and Malenfant covered their tracks by somehow persuading the city police department to hold surrogate hearings on the shooting, hopefully brushing the entire matter under a rug somewhere. Atracura and company had removed Bergeron and Peterson, the two who had attempted to meet with Steve after the shooting.

It all seems perfectly straightforward, except....

Peter Goodman can learn nothing about the other car, the car that is almost like Steve Lansing's. If this is the car that is being used to smuggle false Canadian currency from the states, why is it never seen, never stopped at the border crossing? If this car very simply does not exist, then why was Steve shot at? Why do people claim from time to time to see this red and white Crown Victoria driving late night Windsor Streets?

The truckdriver is another problem. Why is Dolan casually handing out counterfeit bills? Surely if a client has paid him in dross, then that client can be traced through him. Would a client be so foolish? And why has this Dolan not yet been picked up and questioned about his valueless largesse?

There are still too many questions.

Yesterday, Atracura was seen again at his shopping centre pay phones. Goodman will continue attempting to get a tap, although he has to do so discretely through a friend who is in the detective division. He will also continue trying to probe, or as his computer operator friend says, access, the so far apocryphal seeming American computer, just to confirm the truth of the story he has constructed. Random attempts have narrowed drastically the selection of possible locations for the U.S. connection, possibly to a computer in Bethesda, Maryland.

It will never hurt to be sure, says Peter Goodman.

***

On the top floor of the nearly vacant municipal parking garage, a freshly washed white Cadillac convertible reflects the fading rays of the rainswept sun, the blond man at the wheel gazing across the grey concrete wall, across the dismal rain soaked rooftops, across the bloodshot grey mass of border river, across the sunset to somewhere in Missouri, to where another river flows past some old memory.

In the ashen shadows of the opening to the upward ramp a black car materialises, gliding smoothly to the side of its sister Cadillac in the slowly fading light. The driver of the white Eldorado and the driver of the black Seville meet at the midway point between the two cars, and they talk. Then Rudy Noiraud hands Jimmy Dolan a thick brown envelope. Jimmy Dolan returns nothing but his assurance of a job well done.

The contract is sealed. The black car and the white car drive into the deepening grey of Windsor dusk. The sun is setting.

Chapter Forty Three

All week the rain has fallen. Today, after a few early morning exploratory droplets, the skies drew back their drapings of grey to expose a clear blue backdrop for tonight's fiery performance.

Janice Bergeron is again working on a special project. Knowing that she would have to work late, Janice had called Steve earlier in the evening and arranged to meet him in the park. She would drive directly downtown from work.

Steve Lansing had left his apartment shortly after seven thirty, walking the few blocks to the grassy centre of Dieppe Gardens. The fireworks were not scheduled to start until after nine, but Steve had not been certain when Janice would arrive. it was a comfortable night for observing strollers in the park. Steve did not expect to return home until after eleven, since the Festival fireworks normally take about two hours.

Now it is nine thirty. Janice has arrived some time ago. Coloured light has filled the sky for nearly half an hour. A mass of faces inclines heavenward, among them, those of Janice Bergeron and Steve Lansing.

***

Frank Teufel and Les Malenfant are looking not heavenward but down, poring over piles of paper, scanning notebooks and files, newspaper clippings and miscellanea under the half light of pocket flashlights in search of...what?

It has been more than an hour and they have found very little that is useful to them among Steve's disorderly files. On a small bulletin board above the desk is Peter Goodman's name and telephone number. Beside the typewriter is another slip of paper, on which is written the computer entry key for the continental information bank in Washington. Other than that there are just piles of clippings and notes, handwritten and typed, touching on police harassment or brutality plus practically any topic which might possibly relate to the world of organized crime. All that is clear is that Commander Pazitch is correct: Steve Lansing is probing, seekinginformation from any and all sources he can uncover, rooting out information he should not have.

But there is nothing more specific than that.

If it is difficult to tell precisely how much sensitive information Steve Lansing has acquired, it is not difficult to know what headquarters wants done about it. There has been no direct order, but Commander Pazitch has told Frank Teufel he wants the probing stopped. Soon.

This is the next question on the agenda. Teufel and Malenfant must decide how to stop Steve Lansing.

Chapter Forty Four

The telephone is already ringing as Steve fumbles for the door lock in the dark entranceway to his apartment. He wishes he had replaced the overhead bulb before this, rather than waiting for the landlord to take care of it. The telephone is still ringing as he finally opens the door and steps inside. Street lamps insinuate their blue half light through the windows of the apartment, turning it more misty than black. Without searching for light switches, Steve gropes through the living room to the kitchen, where the telephone is still ringing. Half seen hands raise the handset through the blue air.

"Hello?"

"Is that Steve Lansing?"

"Ah, yeah. Who...?"

"I'm a friend. I need some help. Maybe I can help you too."

"What do you mean, help? Who are you? What do you want?"

"It's about your trouble with the cops. I've seen the other car. There are other things I can tell you. Can we meet, tonight?"

"It's almost midnight!"

"It's important."

"You said you need help. What do you want? Who are you?"

"My name's Rick. Rick Bergeron."

"You're crazy! Bergeron's dead!"

"I hope not."

"If you're Bergeron, where have you been?"

"Toronto. Hiding."

"How could I help you?"

"Toronto's no good anymore. I hear you have a cop friend who could maybe help. You know, in trade for information."

"What's your wife's name?"

"Janice."

"Home address?"

"2971 Meadowbrook."

"What kind of information?"

"About Lazlo. About the organization. About that red and white car."

"Where do you want to meet?"

"You know the A & W downtown?"

"Yeah, bottom of Ouellette, about four blocks from here."

"It's usually pretty quiet this time of night. Wait there. I'll find you."

"Now?"

"Please."

Steve suspects a trick of some sort, but his curiosity is piqued. it is unlikely that Rick Bergeron is still alive. But what if he is? And if he is dead, then who would call pretending to be him? A brightly lit fast food restaurant on a well lit street should be safe enough. Steve wants to meet this so called Rick Bergeron face to face.

He retraces his path through the blue haze of the living room, stopping long enough to lock the apartment door behind himself, then he walks down the stairs to the brighter blue of Riverside Drive. He follows Riverside to Ouellette Avenue and turns left. Half a block further he turns into the restaurant and takes a booth near the back, ordering a coffee. He and the two staff are alone.

At twelve o'clock the restaurant is due to close. Steve has finished his coffee. No one else has come in. There is no Rick Bergeron. Steve gets out of the booth and begins his walk home.

A gathering of shadows consolidates itself as Steve approaches a baker's dozen human figures centred on another, wraith of black and white, maestro of the moment. Steve is somehow not surprised to see the young mime still on the nearly empty streets, still plying his timeless profession. He stops a moment in the cool blue summer air to watch the midnight legerdemain.

The white faced enchanter appears to recall Steve, drawing him with a white gloved wave and a flourish, into the circle before turning again to his artistry.

**

The drive home seems interminable to Janice.

She should really have stayed overnight downtown with Steve, but she wants the comfort of a morning shower and clothes selected at leisure, a relaxed beginning to the day ahead. Today has been hectic. In addition to her usual work around the office, she has been working on the special marketing presentation for Mr. Jackson. She began work early and she worked late and still there is more to do before the job is finished. Tomorrow afternoon at three is deadline for the presentation. Janice must go in to work early. And she must go in refreshed.

In fact, Janice had seriously considered staying away from the fireworks tonight, but she had decided that it would not be too tiring to just sit and watch the display with Steve. Now it is almost midnight and she thinks she might after all have been wiser to drive straight home from work. A warm glass of milk and a shot of sherry wrap their peaceful aura around Janice as she sinks in the cotton womb of her bed and the world slips away like some half remembered movie.

**

It is just after midnight and the telephone is ringing. The telephone is still ringing, but at the far end of the line there is no answer. Janice cannot reach Steve.

Chapter Forty Five

The face overwhelms the screen, gargantuan kabuki whiteness filling every corner of a vastness broken only by the black of overthin smiling lips, and the eyes: those warm, lush eyes overflowing with ebony tears that etch a scar the length of each cheek. Janice is mesmerized, watching in fascination as the camera rolls back slowly from the white face of the mime.

Here he is from the waist upward, hands upward, palms forward flat in a Betty Boop Shirley Temple singin' dancin' flourish. There is no music, only a soft hush and crackling like early winter pine warming the room. There is no movement except for an almost imperceptible swaying of the mime form as the camera continues to roll, to expose more and more of the world behind the screen.

The background is beginning to come into focus now, to fill in the void once occupied by the still shrinking mime, to take on form and colour where once the screen was white. The only half clarified world of the mime seems populated by slender, bright strands, perhaps of ribbon, perhaps of tall leaved plants swaying gently in the wind, swaying as the mime sways, softly and hypnotically. The camera keeps rolling, ever backward from the screen.

He has shrunk more, perhaps to life size but from where Janice sits he appears less than half that, and he sways, sways and sways before a wilderness garden of brilliant red and yellow rushes swaying and swaying. He moves like some mythical cobra, hypnotically, suggestively. Cut to camera two.

Cut to Janice. Janice has not expected to get out of her seat this way, not to walk along the long aisle to the front, not to climb the stairs to the front of the stage, not to cross the stage to the screen, not to walk into the world of the silent white faced man in that softly swaying jungle. From here, the screen is suspended across a magenta sky; the image an empty ancient movie theatre with two unmanned cameras in the aisle. It is black and white except for the minute spark of red near the centre, at about where Janice had been seated a few moments before. The red spreads, like blood, like flames, like a flash of light in the night, and the screen is gone. There is only this world of swaying sensuous leaves and the mime.

Janice is at a loss. She has not directed this part of the dream. She sends a visual query to the mime, who reaches behind his ear and from some secret recess withdraws miniatures of two comfortable upholstered armchairs. When he sets them on the ground they grow rapidly to a proper size for sitting. A deep bow, a flourish, a gesture: Janice is invited to sit, and she does.

Another flourish by the white gloved hand and the firmament before them opens like the iris of a camera, outward, forming a circular viewport. They sit like some ancient god and goddess in the clouds, watching the mortal world below their vantage.

Windsor is a miniature city, a child's toy, divided from Detroit by a fine grey painted line river, connected to Detroit by a fine grey painted line bridge. Janice can see everything, can see the riverfront, can see Steve's apartment in minutest detail below her. The white gloved hand points.

The sky below Janice but above the painted river is blooming in all the colours of the rainbow, is becoming a petite aurora borealis, a garden of fire flowers appearing and disappearing in the night. The white gloved hand points.

It is Steve's apartment. It fascinates Janice that she can see the interior of the apartment as though the walls and roof were glass, and yet she cannot see well enough to tell what two men she does not know are doing there with the lights off. The white gloved hand points.

The fireworks are at their zenith, a profusion of colours bursting but becoming obscured as brown clouds of smoke drift across the scene. It should be nearly time for the final production of

143

the evening, the ultimate display the masses along the riverfront have been awaiting. The white gloved hand points.

There is a blond man in Steve's apartment. Is it Steve? The lights are still off. Janice cannot tell. He is doing something in the entrance hallway. Locking the door? Unlocking the door? Janice cannot tell. The white gloved hand points.

The sky is ablaze with man's final great spectacle of pyrotechnics for the evening: American and Canadian flag images enhanced by a variety of smaller surrounding forms. Then the spectacle is over. The sky below goes dark. Janice looks up.

It seems to Janice that the rushes that encompass this clearing are closer now, that their colours are somehow more intense. She turns to ask the mime...the white gloved hand points.

It is Steve's apartment. The blond man is still there. Near his hand is a spot of yellow light, perhaps a flashlight. It is a small ball of light. It is growing, a miniature sun, a room filling blinding glare, a supernova! Nothing. Black smoke obscures the world below. The smoke rises, filling the hole in the firmament, sealing and solidifying. Janice turns toward the mime.

It is almost as though she has entered the gentle jungle. The white faced, white gloved man is gone. In his place is a kindly nearly two dimensional lion figure. Now the rushes are very near, hovering protectively over Janice and her lion. Janice thinks she has seen a painting like this somewhere. It is very placid in the painting and all the gentle, helpless creatures are gathered around the child and the companionable lion. There are no others here, no defenceless creatures. Janice is alone with the lion. Janice remembers the mellow greens of the painted forest. The tall red forms are beginning to bend menacingly over her; the lion is turning Pekinese and irritable. The lion is lapping at her legs. The leaves leap, become flames, lap and linger, threatening incineration. Janice writhes and screams as her clothes burst into flames.

Janice is awake. But she is not at home and it takes her a while to realise where she is
      Steve's apartment
          plaster snake
              errant sunball
                    blackweeping mime
                         golden lion

screaming in the acrid black of night tearing Janice through the back of the screen, into the theatre, into the world! The director's white gloved hand points.

Pan the empty theatre. The house lights are up. The screen is empty. Cut to Janice.

Janice is wide eyed awake, bolt upright in bed, shivering.

She reaches hopefully through the darkness of her bedroom for the bedside lamp. She reaches for the light of the real world. She hopes for the realer light of day.

Chapter Forty Six

UNDERWORLD FIREWORKS ROCK WINDSOR/DETROIT FREEDOM FESTIVITIES

Two Windsor men were killed late yesterday in separate gangland style bombings during and shortly following the evening's fireworks display.

According to Windsor Police, Lucio "Bud" Atracura, 46, a local businessman and transportation entrepreneur, died at approximately 9:30 p.m., when a violent blast destroyed much of his home at 4980 Halston Drive. Although no valuables appeared to have been removed, a wall safe in the house had been forced open.

At about midnight, a second explosion ripped through an apartment above the Riverside Upholstery Company at 321 Riverside Drive East, killing the lone occupant. Although extensive facial damage was sustained in the blast, police have confirmed that the second victim was Stephen Lansing, 29, an unemployed writer who several months ago alleged that Windsor Police constables had fired shots at him.

Subsequent hearings revealed that no firearms had been involved in the incident. Police are unable at this time to determine whether there is any connection between the two bombings, both of which are currently under investigation.

***

TOP PRIORITY
CONFIDENTIAL
CIB: BETHESDA USTF 7601 B2
PLEASE FORWARD ALL AVAILABLE INFORMATION:
LANSING, STEPHEN PERCIVAL
BORN CALGARY, ALBERTA, CANADA, JANUARY 10, 1949
NO KNOWN CRIMINAL RECORD
NOTE: MAY BE A RINGER, TRY ALSO:
DOLAN, JAMES WILLIAM
BORN CEDAR CITY, MISSOURI, U. S. A., MARCH 13, 1950
SEVERAL WANTS OUTSTANDING, MISSOURI ORIGIN
CORRELATE IF POSSIBLE
END OF COMMUNICATION
PAZITCH, CMDR XNTF 3851 B1

Chapter Forty Seven

It had seemed a dream. The fireball had burst from the bay window like the sun itself, lighting the streets for blocks. Columns of black smoke and licking, lapping flames had chased behind. The roof had lifted slightly. The tremendous sound had reached out to snap Steve around to face the spectacle. Steve had stood unable to move and had watched it all. It had seemed a dream: all of it in slow motion. By the time he thought again to look around himself, there were people running everywhere. He had not realised until later that the mime and his audience had gone.

Steve had walked south on Ouellette Avenue and had hailed a cab.

***

It has been three days since the explosion. Janice Bergeron has taken the time off work. She has not left her townhouse since Steve came that early morning and told her what had happened. Steve and Janice have been waiting. All the lights are out except the one beside the bed. It is two in the morning.

"Steve?"

"I'm here."

"Do you hear something? Outside?"

"Only the wind."

"I'm cold."

They lay in silence, waiting for sleep that does not want to come. They move closer to each other in the night.

"There! Do you hear it?"

"I'll take a look."

"Steve. Don't go."

"I heard it too. Downstairs. I'll just check."

"Don't. Please?""It's probably nothing. I'll be careful. I'll be back right away. Wait."

"I'll come with you."

Janice is with Steve as he walks slowly, quietly down the stairs and turns the corner to enter the living room. The only sounds now are the slight whisper of wind and an occasional night bird calling. Softly, Janice touches Steve's shoulder and without a word they stop.

The patio door stands open, slid nearly all the way, the breeze playing with the sheer drapes that dance gently in and out of the room. It is peaceful: not a sound now within the house. Janice eases past Steve as though to slip the door closed.

"Steve?" She is through the doorway, into the yard beyond. Steve follows her into the darkness.

Chapter Forty Eight

The sun rising.

A hunch.

Just past darkness, all is quiet now in the house. On this morning of the third day since the fireworks spread their rainbow high above the river between two nations, all seems as it should be.

There is light shining from an upstairs window. Her car sits in front, the engine cold. The doorbell brings no answer. The door eases open at the touch of a hand, as though left slightly ajar in welcome.

"Hello!"

The call, hello a second time, rolls around the walls and in upon itself. In the kitchen, the half empty coffee pot is still plugged in—it seems to hear and chuffs a cheery welcome.

The kitchen is empty.

New sunlight floods the living room through the sliding glass doors, bringing a visual warmth to the chill of morning in this empty room.

Up the stairs a third hello rolling ahead unheard or unanswered.

The chill hangs on here, although the sun is beginning to fill and warm the emptiness.

The lamp is on in the front bedroom. Blankets thrown off at an angle from rumpled sheets, cold now. Two pillows: two impressions. On the tables, a coffee cup half emptied and one almost full.

Downstairs in the kitchen with a coffee, Goodman waits. They cannot be gone long or far.

Outside, the shadows sink eastward into the earth, only to reappear in the western haze as the growing dark.

Goodman waits.

The western sky burns red, and still he waits, watching from the upstairs window as the sun sets.

FIN

Canadian novelist, poet, arts reviewer, and performer Bob MacKenzie has been writing poetry, fiction, arts commentary and criticism, and songs since 1965. Reflection, his first book of poetry, was published in 1965.

Bob's poetry has been widely published in newspapers, magazines, journals and anthologies across Canada and The United States, and worldwide; including, with noted Canadian printmaker G. Brender à Brandis, five of his poems as signed and numbered limited edition prints and a limited edition art-book, The Little Song (1975). Bob has also released six albums of spoken word and songs with the performance group Poem de Terre, including War & Love (2006); and published five more books between 2007 and 2012.

Bob's prose and poetry has received a number of awards, including an Ontario Arts Council grant for literature, and the Canada Council's National Art Bank has several visual arts representations of his poetry.

Dark Matter Press
Kingston Ontario
A Canadian Publisher

Author biography by Dorothyanne Brown
Biography updated by the author
Author photograph by Annie MacKenzie

www.ingramcontent.com/pod-product-compliance
Lightning Source LLC
Chambersburg PA
CBHW020700030726
47498CB00002B/583